Us He Devours

Us He Devours

by James B. Hall

New Directions — San Francisco Review

For Walter and Paul—
    good teachers, good men

Some of the stories in this book first appeared in the following magazines: *A.A.U.P. Bulletin, The Carleton Miscellany, Epoch, Esquire, Furioso, Harper's Bazaar, North American Review, Northwest Review, Perspective, San Francisco Review,* and *Western Review.*

Published simultaneously in Canada by McClelland & Stewart, Ltd.

Manufactured in the United States of America.

New Directions Books are published by James Laughlin at Norfolk, Connecticut. New York Office: 333 Sixth Avenue (14).

Contents

Us He Devours

Us He Devours

The goat coughed in the tree outside her window.

Oh she had waited so long to see the hoofs firm upon the lowest branches, the flanks slender, stretched upward among the catalpa leaves, the head half concealed, the backward curving horns erect, glistening in the moist light of the moon.

Miss Festner had thought all these times were past, forever, but now her branches rustled louder, and she stiffened in her bed. Stringy and coarse and rancid as a chicken house floor, the odor afloat in the catalpa tree came to her. She lay in her bed and she felt her back and her thighs harden. This time she was determined to wait.

From experience Miss Festner knew that to leap from her bed, to rush to the casement, to cry out, was useless. When younger she had cried out, in fear; later she knew she must wait without emotion. Not always did the goat leap with a terrible cracking of small branches, and scramble pawing across her window sill.

Sometimes it came—perhaps silently—then deserted her. Sometimes the cry of reed pipes swelled inside her room until

3

her ears and heart and her hard breasts ached; sometimes, after the cry of the loon and after the last crackling noise of great weight among branches, it went away. If it awakened her, and then deserted her, she would go to her window and stare out across the town, which fell away below her windows toward the river. Therefore she did not now dare look toward the window when the odor of stalls and rabbit hutches and stables came to her like smoke from the leaves of the shimmering tree.

For this it seemed she had been waiting a very long time. She had almost given up hope, but now she did what she could. Her quick money-counting fingers dug deeper into the little holes in the farthest edges of her mattress. The sheet across her knees and thighs and her dry belly made spasms of motion.

Some things she could not control, but some things she could do: always she left her window open, she used only the lightest of sheets, and always she was *clean, clean*. If she looked now the eyes she might see would flee into the kingdom of her dreams. But oh tonight she could not wait.

With her eyes still closed she threw the small sheet from her body. Exposed. Yes and on display and naked as the first day her quick money-counting fingers worked inside her Teller's cage. From Escrows in the bank, she had gone behind a Teller's window. Since then she had her window at the bank, with bars, and the businessmen of the town came to her with money and she handled each day the hard, hand-fitting, phallic rolls of dimes, nickels, and quarters. That night in spring, for the first time, the goat coughed in the catalpa tree in the yard of her small house and in her inexperience and her fear she had run too quickly to her bedroom window and the musk-scented thing had fled somewhere across the roiled shadows of her yard.

Finally she learned to wait motionless in her bed, for only then would the wool-soft yarn and the perfume and the polished mother-of-pearl horns and the soft resilient body— only then would it stay lovely as flowers unfolding beside and over her until the dawn humming awoke in her arms. Those mornings she telephoned Mr. Nelscot at the bank. She did not go down the hill to sit behind the window of her Teller's cage until after her lunch.

Louder now outside her bedroom window the small branches shattered. Was now the time, this night?

In the catalpa tree outside she heard it whet the saber of its horns against the topmost branches. Were the hoarse violent eyes staring at her now?

She resisted a moment, and then she no longer cared. To see, to glimpse it among branches seemed enough. She opened wide her eyes.

No. Not there. Gone.

The cry of the loon in the frozen trees chilled her. She had been terribly hot; now she was not hot. She felt more deserted, and more forlorn, than ever before. Yet she was not and never could be sinfully passive, for urgency even in her waking hours grew like a fuse somewhere inside her. She recognized, she even welcomed, the desperation that came galloping to her. She knew she must go out, must seek, must search once more.

Of late when the goat coughed in the branches outside her window and then deserted her, she had followed. Once she had been astonished at her own headlong urgency, but she had gone on because she believed that in frenzy was the hot little kernel of satisfaction. Now that restraint was somewhere far behind her she could think of nothing at all except a highway, twisting somewhere ahead.

II

Furiously she drove the country, limestone roads. Ahead on a curve the guardrails writhed in her headlight beams. At a crossroad she saw the shadow of a country mailbox lie black beside some farmer's lane, and as she passed the black check mark shadow seemed to fade, and then to become a check mark of flame in the corner of her headlong eye.

The constant search, it was, that vexed her. At one time the first place she stopped was always the right place. But as the years fled her, she found the right place was now always farther away, until now she was resigned to the longest drive of all: this night she knew without caring that she would go far beyond a familiar tilt-roofed, ramshackle barn that roosted in a pasture, reviled even by the shoat's moist farming nose.

One spring she had first gone outside. She had gone directly to a certain creek that divided two meadows, where a sand bar of supine luminous tissues of gravel lay exposed between rocks and the water. Later she found her sand bar was not the right place and she had to drive on to a field freshly harrowed, and then on still farther, in the fall, to a place of stubbles, of wheat lately under the sickle bars of harvest. From habit, or from some terrible wish, she still drove first to the sand bar and then to the fields, in the order of their discovery. Finally she came to a familiar bridge. Across this bridge was a grove of oaks that was lovely and dark and deep, a mat of green between two hills.

The planks of the bridge seemed to say this was the place that she must find. But she could accept no comfort from the mutter of planks. Always, until the final moment, there was uncertainty. Suppose the place now had to be still more remote, a place where she could never travel, a place so cleverly concealed in a shaggy-thighed wood that no one could ever find it. She could not think upon that ultimate possibility. As always, at this time, she knew with the Bible-black certainty of prayer that here was the place. Here nothing would be denied her.

The boxes and packages she kept locked in the car trunk. These were things she bought on impulse during her lunch hour or on Saturday, as though each purchase were for herself. She had not thought there were so many, but the oblong, white boxes and the largest flat box—all of them—seemed to leap into her arms. Without pausing she ran across a culvert and across a flat small meadow and into the first sentinel trees at the oak grove's edge.

Too late she realized the briers also guarded the grove. They had grown and had become heavy as barbed wire since the last time.

With the white boxes held high above her head, and with her robe open, flapping behind her, she leaped high and for a moment seemed to float above the caress of briers. She landed running. Her legs burned. But Miss Festner did not cry out.

Ahead she saw the smooth arena, in the center of her secret grove of oaks.

"Here, oh here," she said to the briers, which seemed to roll away in unbroken humps of light toward a creek beyond.

"Here. I am here, now," she said to the crossed branches of the trees overhead. "Here . . ."

She took off her robe.

She spread the robe near the boxes, at the edge of the clearing. Carefully in the moonlight she searched the clay ground, inch by inch; there was no dung, and no hair of cattle wedged in the bark of the oak trees. As she had imagined as she drove those limestone roads, the grove was clean, clean.

In the middle of the hoof-packed clay in the center of the grove of oaks, Miss Festner lay herself down upon the ground, which now seemed warm under the muscles of her flesh.

Nothing did come to her.

She was alone.

She listened but she heard only the mockery of silence among the trunks of trees. The intricate thunder of possibility shook her: was this the end, was she to be deserted like this at the final meeting place between two hills.

Then she heard it cough.

Nearby in the encircling brier she heard its jaws nibble the harsh vegetation. A small branch ripped under the plunge of a hoof. Then she heard it above her, high in the canopy of branches overhead; perhaps it was now looking down at the raised, white supplication of her arms.

She heard once more the cry of the loon: near, then far away. She heard something hoarse, and very close, in the ring of the briers. Held fast in the bondage of her desire, she lay with eyes closed in the moonlight, and still nothing came to her.

Over, she thought. Oh over and gone and never again to return to me. She realized a truth about herself: since the first time when the hair was sweet as a cloud of wool above her she had given more and more of herself. She had walked much, had driven farther and farther into strange woods. Then, like a reprieve, the coarse odor came to her. The lust of its eye rustled the briers.

The gifts. Yes, the boxes piled near her robe. Each time, with gifts, she also gave more and more. At first it was only a flower tossed lightly upon the sand bar. Then her gifts were only the green enticement, but finally she had to give the silks of reward, everything. . . .

In a frenzy she opened her gifts.

Against rocks she broke the expensive, sullen perfumes. Each vial shattered and split and this enticement by odor overwhelmed even the trunks of the black trees.

Oh, come to me?

She paused, listened.

Somewhere beyond the shadows, somewhere in the forest of that night she felt something advance. She felt something come closer to her.

Her quick money-counting fingers clawed at the smaller boxes. She ripped tissue paper from all the jewels she had purchased at all the big jewelry stores all across the city. Tiaras and small rings and pearls in white strands, all these she tore into shreds of diamonds and single rubies and broken pearls, and these she threw into the encircling briers.

Oh, come to me?

The odor—so lurid, so near—seemed to stroke her thighs, and then in the old way it seemed to retreat beyond her farthest gifts.

Without her seeming to touch the hoof-packed clay she ran to the largest, final package. This she had saved, for the habit of frugality could also be with her, even in moments of extravagance.

She opened the box. The white, intense fleece of a lamb was what she held aloft. She waved the fleece in the light of the clearing. She held the fleece above her lowing mouth. She allowed the fleece to fall like a shower of myrrh and spice, to fall like the color of flowers around her, to cover her shoulders and her back with the incense of new wool.

Oh, come to me?

When nothing came to her, Miss Festner ran toward the thing she heard, toward a harsh plunging noise, in those final briers.

But she stopped. She knew it had deceived her, and therefore she stood weeping and ruined, fanned by the hot cry of the loon, in the center of briers and all her nights.

III

Escrow, Checking, Loans, and finally a Teller's cage: she had worked through each department, and now as the green floodgate doors of the bank opened, promptly at ten, she watched people swim into the bright hard marble pool of light, the interior of First National, Main.

In the hard security of a Teller's cage, she began this day by loosening the green drawstrings of green moneybags. Rolls of coins were what she found in each puffy little sack, rolls of dimes, and quarters, and half dollars, each roll made especially for her hand. In even rows the packets of bills, the twenties and fifties, fit precisely into each slot of her tray, and she felt the first smile of the morning hazard its first trial with the flesh of her own lips and cheeks as a customer snuffled just beyond the bars of her window.

From up the line, from Window Number One, Miss Festner heard the money-counting sound of laughter. The sound of the laughter made her see the two derby hats and the two false beards of the two men who were shaking hands with a Vice-President in the officers' enclosure, across the room. When she also saw the two beards rise and fall with the handshakes of the two men, she felt her own mouth pick up the laughter and pass it on to the next Teller in the long, money-counting line.

The State's Centennial Year, it was. The State Banking Inspectors were making believe. Across the room, in the officers' marble enclosure, two short men in make-believe beards began to laugh and laugh.

While her fingers counted out sixty-nine-sixty of a pensioner's check, which had snuffled under the bars of her window, she knew the ledgers and the adding machine tapes folded and held with paper clips and the dormant accounts and the Escrows were writhing, somewhere in the vaults or the storage rooms of First National, Main Branch.

Though the bills and the coins flowed through and around and over her fingers as water flows over and around a sand bar in some moonlit creek, the two derby hats and the beards of false gray hair seemed to float, seemed to become an echo, in the high corners of the main floor.

The edges of marble, the parallel shadows on the foot-trampled floor, the parallel lines of the brass-barred window before her, were the squares and the bars of a place she clearly remembered.

Across the bridge, beyond the village edge, was where the pens were. There in Ohio, beyond the edge of a limestone road, she had awakened from the sleepless dawns of girlhood to hear the cruel roosters cry *blood*, *blood*, *bloooood* across the sties and pens and across the hen yard's dusty wallows. Often she lay in her bed, listening to the sounds of animals already awake; the snigger of boars or somewhere in the corner of a pasture the dry dirt-pawing hoof of her father's bull. The dirt, the droppings of turkeys and pea fowl, and the dung of sparrows on a beam under the barn's eave were always there, or were seen in memory only as a brown composite of wind and random dust flapping across barnyards.

In that house the women swept floors, brushed crumbs from tables, rocked toward evening, waited for the odor of farm boots and the odor of work clothes, denim jackets, and

old felt hats to walk through kitchen doors; waited until the
warm odor of milk drifted into the fried heat of a kitchen in
March.

In summer a tomcat lolled on the tendrils and the matted
leaves of a grape arbor, and stared all day at the martin's box
high on a curved, white pole.

Mostly she remembered the things maimed: a rabbit leap-
ing from stubble into the light of her father's sickle bar;
the cut-shoat's lyric scream; the pullet, headless toward noon,
butting a post of her mother's clothesline. Or the hired men,
their fingers aligned at the thresher's dinner table, each man
with something clipped off, missing: a finger gone to the nibbling belt of a corn sheller, a toe left at a chopping block, a
hand or a forearm shucked by the whirling, frost-wet picker
rolls.

All of that was past. She had gone to school, though she
had visited her old home out of sentiment at the change of
each season. For three years she taught at a consolidated high
school. Though she tried to beat them with a yardstick the
hulking baseball and football and basketball players refused
to obey her. Finally the principal said why after all the First
National, Main, paid twice as much, and then she could really
have a place of her own. Therefore she had gone to live at the
edge of this town, where sometimes a goat coughed in the
catalpa leaves, and the backward curve of horn was mother-
of-pearl in the moist light of the moon.

The two Inspectors came back toward noon.

Finally they began to work. Because it really was the Centennial Year, they wore derby hats and gray, false whiskers
while they walked in and out of the officers' marble enclosure,
or in and out of the vaults. She heard them laughing as they
worked, and from her window it seemed they walked through
the glass partitions. Toward three o'clock they walked past,
together, nibbling a candy bar with their white goat teeth;
and then they were behind the row of Tellers, nibbling stacks
and stacks of twenties and fifties with their money-counting
fingers.

At four o'clock doors were locked and the blinds were drawn, and only the feet and the knees of people walked past in the disembodied street. When she saw the legs walking past, Miss Festner thought, Why yes, tomorrow or the next day some one of the officers will walk up behind me and will stare and will then walk away as though he had seen something different. Then she would say what she knew all the others like her always said to the press: For my friends, for my friends, I did it, because I wanted them to be as happy as I have always been. You see, I gave it all to my friends . . .

At check-out, in the steel-lined vault, she saw the other money trays, all in a row. She knew this might be her last night at home in her own bed, in the room where the catalpa leaves were sometimes perfume in the night.

For the last time, tonight, she knew she might hear the hoofs firm upon the lowest branches, might see the flanks slender, stretched upward among the leaves, and might see also that final, unwinking eye stare at her from the tenderness of leaves.

Without hesitation she opened her massive, over-the-shoulder purse. Into the wide unlatched maw she stuffed all the singles and bundles of twenties and bundles of fifty dollar bills that her country hands could gather. In case, oh, in case it was money that was wanted, after all.

As always, Mr. Nelscot was standing at the bank door.

He smiled and he bowed very slightly as he let Miss Festner and her valise of a purse out the door.

All over again she heard the click of the door of First National, Main, behind her. She knew he would never do more than smile, would never do more than bow ever so slightly as he opened the door for her to leave. Or had that been his voice, after all; had he said as she left, as the door shut and clicked somewhere in the past and also in the future of her days, had he said too late, "See you. Same time tomorrow?"

In the Eye of the Storm

In the Eye of the Storm

Shall I keep ringing that number?

Their washer was gone. The hot and cold water hoses were melted gun barrels pointing into the utility room floor. In the kitchen their refrigerator had left an oblong of gray lint on the floor but the mixer and juicer and electric knife sharpener were still on the Formica counters. Depford knew the installers and the men taking other appliances away had milled through the house, getting in each other's way. And now his wife was also gone.

In the bedroom Depford found nothing at all. The night stand, radio, her records, the bed, and the water cooler were gone. By now Depford could not remember exactly which items he had ordered sent from the stores and which items he had traded in as down payments. This new disorder was at once complete and yet vacant but Depford believed he had it all recorded on sales slips in his pockets—a separate pocket in his clothes for each room in this re-echoing house, here in the uninflected smoky night of their suburb.

Depford could imagine it well enough. Louise was all right except when people came and took away things from the bedroom. Probably the bedroom people arrived and took everything just at the moment the new things arrived. It was enough to make Louise leave once again. Depford knew she had called a taxi, or to save them money she might have ridden back to the YWCA on top of a van.

So there was nothing to do except sit in the corner of the bedroom and listen to the sand from the plaster grind between his coat and the bedroom walls as he moved his shoulders up and down, trying to sleep until morning.

Please, no dancing! per your Host.

. . . Not dawn nor the silver lining, but rain spoke the window pane: excelsior, brown paper, and the corrugated boxes outside popped and fried in the darkness. Depford could barely move because of the stiffness in his legs, and across the whole terrace of the suburb no lights came on but angora tails of smoke showed the thermostats had awakened to this first freshet of winter. Outside in the drizzle Depford tried to find the small boxes. Some firms had made delivery and had left things at the front door while he slept. A pile of large boxes and crates were astride the front walk—a half-dozen shipments. The porch light was no help, and then the larger crates began to swell in the cold rain.

When Depford tried to lift the big crates, he felt sleet on his back. Then he remembered the tarpaulins in the cellar. Once Depford had written copy on a tarpaulin deal. Maybe he wrote too well.

By the time he staked down the tarps it was beginning to get light. He knew the agency would be expecting him and he had the premonition they might just fire him this time. Therefore he stopped worrying about the crates astride the front walk and about Louise for he really wanted to shave and to get back to work after this buying spree. But they had taken his razor and his mirror when they took the medicine cabinet off the wall of the bathroom, and now their new medicine cabinet was still outside, staked down under a quarter inch of sleet, but he had no record in any of his pockets. Finally it was really morning.

She wants the baby—doctors won't let her.

At the agency, Depford's head was on the desk when they fired him.

At two o'clock he opened one eye just as the check was slipped under his arm, very near his half-parted lips. While he was cleaning out his desk the Copy Chief came up and slapped him on the back and said those old papers could wait. Said Mr. Willer wants very much to speak to you.

Willer was Vice-President and could not understand all of this. Now what about all of this? Hated it, of course, but when there is no recourse then there is no recourse. Do you not agree Dep, Old Sod?

Depford said he did agree. Depford supposed he should attend more to business instead of walking out to lunch with all the carbons of his own ad copy. Of course he did call back that one time and the Copy Chief had said . . .

"Cer-tain-ly," Mr. Willer broke in. "No areas of disagreement in your case need be defined, Dep Old Sod."

The Copy Chief sat on a stool in the corner.

At lunch Willer had stated he wanted to get to the bottom of this, and so the Copy Chief wanted to listen.

"As I would see it, Dep Old Sod," Willer said, "what you would need is a budget."

Mr. Willer began to draw lines on a piece of paper.

"Let's say you get another job at Ten. Suppose twenty per cent goes to the shelter. Now then . . ."

Depford could not follow it.

Around their house were a great many budgets. Some of them had been filled out for six weeks. The white sheet of

Mr. Willer's budget reminded Depford of the sleet that came down like chips of porcelain, and still he had not found where Louise was hiding.

"Give away, to keep up with the down Jones," Mr. Willer seemed to be saying. "But remember: stanff cane. Ladenoff, and makes sense, huh?"

Yes, except the Copy Chief wanted to say a few words at this time. Copy agreed with Willer, but also wanted to point out—for the record—there was no request for stuff by Old Dep on new model cars. Old Dep had imagined that assignment. So to speak had therefore assigned the copy to himself. Surely?

The Copy Chief sat back down on his stool.

Then Mr. Willer wanted to say a few words to back up what had just been said. While Willer and Copy talked at each other Depford remembered how he had come here in the first place. In high school each afternoon he read dictionaries, as a hobby; he tried to find words like "gonad." In class or in study hall he heard what everyone said and on tests he wrote what he heard and that was always enough. His mother and father were both schoolteachers and because they had no children they took over Depford from a local attorney. Depford believed this was true, but he did not believe it was public knowledge. One spring he won the jingle contest and was summoned to this agency to receive his prize and to hear his entry set to music. For the second contest he submitted an entry that was still being played on radio stations in the south. After that everyone said Depford should go into advertising. And so Willer gave him a desk and a cubicle all his own.

But after they had been married nine months, Louise knew something was wrong. Professionally. She understood Depford had to write directly from the product: had to write while staring at a bottle of Sweet-Mo or an illuminated plastic worm for night fishing. The Copy Chief said this realism would take him far. Louise was the first to know how far sincerity would take him when a case of double-ended toothpicks were delivered to the door. That day in their basement she found other things Depford had written about, and had then bought: tarpaulins and a blue, polished, felt-lined box of veterinarian tools. That same day Depford brought home a second car. Willer had assigned second-car copy the week before.

"Whisky I could understand," Louise said. "Or horses or maybe women. I could even understand gardening."

Then he wrote about and had to purchase a folded-up, plastic wading pool. It was delivered in midwinter. For the first time, the next afternoon, Louise left him. . . .

Mr. Willer stood up. Yes, Depford could go now, could go find Louise. Had this little session helped? The Copy Chief said he thought it certainly had helped.

Everyone stood up and everyone shook hands and everyone said, "Good luck to you."

Depford believed he was finished. He was what every advertisement and every agency assumed: the perfect customer, the man who believed what he read. Except Depford was a more pure type than any imagined customer, for he had to believe to produce copy in the first place. And he could not resist what he had himself written. There was no disbelief in him; he wrote himself into poverty. He was paid for sincerity, but he was known as a fool. Because he was innocent all this was kept from him. People stopped talking when he walked past. Consequently he was very much in debt to every client of Willer's agency, because everything he bought was on credit. But now he would go find his wife.

No deposits; no returns.

The desk admitted Louise was back at the Y. True, Louise had been to the movies all day and all yesterday but she would *not* be in until after the last show.

Finally after the desk at the Y was closed for the night Depford drove past the shopping centers to the edge of town.

Louise had not fooled him by sneaking back during the day.
She really was at the movies. The crates from the last shipments were also gone. The tarps were folded and stacked.
Everything that had been outside was now installed, or nailed
up or tacked down. Her new kitchen was a four-color spread,
and Depford knew she would like it if she would only come
home. Had they really forwarded his messages to her room at
the YWCA?

At the rear of their house, Depford saw the empty crates
and boxes and excelsior piled higher than the roof. The neighbors would complain after they saw the first rat.

In the center of the living room floor, sleep took him. Depford had been awake nearly two days. Without thinking anything at all he felt himself spreading out, all parts of his
body bearing an equal weight in the center of a new carpet.
He buttoned his coat around his neck and breathed deeply,
much like a stonemason's apprentice breathes deeply on a
pile of old cement bags at noon after his first morning's work.
Then the telephone rang. It was Louise.

Louise was calling from the YWCA. Louise had an idea.

Keep smiling: there is no time like the pleasant.

Before he could turn the motor off, or could doze off to sleep,
Louise ran down the steps of the YWCA and got in beside
him in their car. Louise was crying a little.

Louise said she could not sleep at the YWCA. She knew she
ought to be more brave and more understanding. She said she
would never leave him again and she kissed Depford very
tenderly.

Depford told her it was all right. Now everything was
installed and the new kitchen was a real dream.

About the idea: Louise said her idea came from the radio at
the YWCA. She had heard a message, so could he try to find
Consolidate?

They had to get to Consolidate before ten o'clock. After

Louise parked their car in front of the loan building she had
to wake Depford once more.

Mr. Lookey was there. Pronounced "Lucky" he said. Offered them cigars, and two packs of gum. "Problem you got;
problem we . . . now what is this all about anyhow?"

Louise began with how they met. She had been traveling
through this small town. There was a street fair. A man had
put them in the same seat of "The Bug." They fell in love.
. . . Then Louise came to the part about the agency, and how
she had to work all the time, too. Of course she liked to work
because they could have the things they ought to have. Finally
she told Mr. Lookey about the Copy Chief.

The Copy Chief had given the House Beautiful copy to
Depford on purpose, as a kind of office joke.

Mr. Lookey said, "Yes, indeed, You are only young once.
Now let's proceed."

He got out a pad of paper and drew some lines on it.

"Young fellow," he said, "you wake up here and give me
the answers."

And then to her, "The management of money is the key to
happiness."

Mr. Lookey asked them how much would they make if the
two of them kept right on working, here at the peak of prosperity, for one year? And how much, since prosperity was
going to get more so, would together they make in twenty-
one years? Finally Mr. Lookey ripped off the page from his
scratch pad. "Now makes sense, does it not?"

Louise said it did. Mr. Lookey said, "Yus, does."

Outside the neon sign flashed back through the window,
"etadilosnoC, etadilosnoC."

The glass brick front with the angle window and the planting of dwarf evergreens looked out upon streetcar tracks.
The trolley cables intersected above the street in exact squares
against the sky. As Mr. Lookey spoke the rain came down
into the street once more, and pecked away at the glass brick
of the front. Somewhere among the planted bed of geraniums,

inside, the transformer for the Consolidate neon hummed like a winter bug in the first hours of hibernation.

Mr. Lookey said, "We buy payments. That's business. You then pay my firm a lump sum each month. Pay one instead of many little litt-le payments. We don't care if you two have jobs or not. You are Youth, and wide-open, U.S. double A. That's our security. Is it not?"

Mr. Lookey said he wanted them to have cash. He signed the papers after they signed. He went to the safe, and the door swung open very easily.

Louise and Depford got back in the car once more. Depford felt better, and so did Louise. He straightened up and began to sing about the good old summer time. Before she could drive away, however, Mr. Lookey had closed the loan office. It was almost midnight, but Mr. Lookey was standing on the curb, tapping on the windows of their car.

"Only young once," he said. "Have a good time!"

Because it was so late and because Depford had been going nearly three days, they decided on a motel. They would drive out to the bungalow tomorrow afternoon, when tomorrow came.

For professional services: well visit. Remit, please.

When they again opened their eyes the snow was in drifts outside the motel windows. Depford telephoned a restaurant for sandwiches. Everything was so warm they stayed another day, listening to the radio, and wondering when the snow would cease to fall. They missed her records and the water cooler, but they talked over everything several times. Finally when Depford had dozed one more day, he awakened, and got up, and began to walk up and down the room of their motel unit. It was time to leave.

On the way home, on top of the last rise of ground, they parked for a minute to look down upon the suburb that was held in the jawbone of a frozen river. She asked him why the igloo?

Depford said it was crates in their back yard.

Louise said it didn't matter. Everything was really all right now.

When the sun lowered itself into a cloud bank, Depford drove on down the hill, letting the car feel its way through the drifts of evening.

Inside the bungalow there was nothing at all.

Everything, every single thing, was gone. Again.

Louise began to cry.

She went up to the bare walls and touched them with the ends of her long fingers. She ran into the bedroom. By accident, the people repossessing things had forgotten their bed. She threw herself on it and pulled her knees up very close to her chin.

Depford walked through all the rooms. He could hear her sobbing a little.

Depford wandered into the utility room. A hose from their old automatic washer was once more a melted gun barrel, pointed at the floor. In the center of the utility room was a scarlet outboard motor. He could not remember writing any copy about that. Perhaps the Copy Chief had played a little joke on them. Depford did not know.

Now everything in the kitchen that had been newly installed before Louise called from the YWCA was gone: the knife sharpener, the toaster, the juicer, the grater, the slicer. Even the new refrigerator had been taken from them before frost collected on metal coils. Only a red plaid clock hung on the kitchen wall. Depford plugged in the cord and stood for two minutes watching the scarlet second hand.

In the bedroom Louise was crying a little bit as she worked at putting on two clean sheets.

Depford tried to put his arm around her, but she twisted away. She did not want to be touched—not ever touched— by anyone. After the bed was made, Louise got in without taking off her shoes.

Depford sat in the corner a long time.

While they were two days at the motel, the vans no doubt came back. A van must have appeared out of the dark, and backed up to the front door. By now everything he had bought on his last big shopping tour was buried in a warehouse near the river, with other lots of used furniture and unclaimed freight, and scrap metal from crashed airplanes.

Something like that, or was this all a mistake? Perhaps someone forgot to write "thirty days" in a blank; perhaps one blank in all those papers was never filled out in the first place. . . .

Near midnight Louise smelled smoke. Somewhere against the wall, where his face was, she saw his cigarette burning. Louise got out of bed and came over to him and took his hands. She sat on the floor beside him and kissed him very tenderly. Louise said it was all right. It was no mistake of his. It was her idea to Consolidate everything. She, herself, had heard the message over the radio.

She said, finally, it was that Mr. Lookey all right.

Depford had known this all along.

Then who is our next president?

After broad daylight the warehouse auctioneers sold everything Depford had dredged up from the basement: the tarpaulins, the veterinarian's tools, the double-ended toothpicks. In fact the outboard motor went for much more than half of what it cost, for the crate was still undamaged.

When Depford returned home and plugged in a new little radio, and when the music came on, Louise felt much better.

Louise opened cans and put the soup on a two-burner hot plate. This was very good, for stored away in their own basement were at least two more automobile loads. They could live out of their own basement—almost like savings—until spring, or even into early summer.

Together they sat on the bed eating their soup from cans.

Depford said absolutely everything they really needed was within easy reach: the new hot plate, the radio. They could block off the rest of the house, and would not see or feel the empty rooms. In fact, she said their bedroom was much like a good motel unit, except they had cooking privileges.

The white sheets of the bed, the white walls, and beyond the windowpanes was the bright, leveling snow. Depford said the two of them, alone in the bedroom, were in some kind of pure state also, as though they consciously had been seeking just that. What they had purchased was gone. What they owned was consolidated. What had been repossessed by the vans had gone for interest in advance, and all the carrying charges. Consequently what they now owed was for the things he bought the day he walked out of the agency without telling the Copy Chief. Louise did not understand this, but she said they could now live within their means, at least, and this was something like a budget.

After lunch they lay side by side on the bed. They were talking about jobs, and how Mr. Willer would soon eat lunch again with the Copy Chief. The Copy Chief would call on the telephone and say something about "obligation," and "old time's sake," and so on. They were considering what should be said in return when their doorbell rang.

Before it rang again, Depford ran upstairs to hide.

Louise opened the door.

At the curb she saw the two blue coupés, parked, their motors feeding. The coupés were parked side by side, as though they traveled in pairs. The two drivers had walked side by side up to the door of the bungalow.

The two men were in identical pearl-gray Homburgs and black coats with pearl-gray felt on the collars. They looked so much alike that she was surprised to see two sets of black footprints leading to the front steps.

The man who was left-handed took off his Homburg. His hair was gray but with streaks of black near the roots much like a woman's hair after she has fixed herself up to work when the ad suggests applicants be "dignified." Before either of the men had a chance to speak, Louise said to them very firmly through her crack in the door:

"Nothing wrong here."

The man who had rung the doorbell was also the most agile. He stepped forward and put his face very close to the crack in the door.

He smiled.

"I'm from Mr. Lookey. The Firm gave me your address on a card. Mr. Lookey says give you best regards. Mr. Lookey says, 'Have a good time.' "

Then the man who was left-handed, and who had rung the doorbell, put his hat back on his gray hair and turned and walked briskly to his coupé and drove away, still smiling a lucky smile.

The other man in an identical pearl-gray Homburg sidled close enough to hear it all. He was a listener. He was not a talker. He looked a little surprised and backed off a step or two when she looked at him. It was as though someone in the home office had unreasonably or mistakenly sent both men on another useless errand. Always they were sent to the same addresses, but they were never allowed to work together. Of course they never spoke, except at banquets.

"Business," he told Louise. "With Depford."

"Not here," she said, as though to drive the man away. "Out of town!"

As Louise shouted through her crack in the door, the man stepped back another step. Deliberately he looked across the upstairs windows.

Behind a dormer, he saw Depford's face. He pointed his finger toward the window, and said something like, "Ah, ha!"

Then he kicked at the footprints in the snow, and pointed a rolled-up envelope at Depford's face behind the windows.

Then the man stood beside his dented blue coupé. He turned once more as though to fix the location of this house exactly in his mind. He was very interested in their bedroom. He had the look of someone who might come back very soon, probably after dark. He stamped his foot in the snow and waved at the dormer window and said something to the snow.

Without hesitation he got into the car, and without sliding or spinning a wheel, he followed the track of the other car and like an apparition, vanished around the corner.

Depford and Louise ran outside.

What the man in the coupé said to the snow seemed to hover close to the frozen ground, as though his threat or his message remained frozen and suspended in the motionless air of their yard. What the words might be they could not say: "See you in church," or, "See you in court," or, "See you, see you, see you."

They faced each other in the cold air and they listened very carefully, but their ears could not know.

Together they walked back into the house.

Depford sat once more in the corner with the sand from the plaster rubbing into his shoulders. Louise felt like going to bed, but she stopped at the packing box chifforobe to see if there was any music on the radio.

Some music would do them both good, and besides the sun had not yet even begun to set.

The Gambler: A Portrait of the Writer

The Gambler: A Portrait of the Writer

On the Ohio side of the river under the Suspension Bridge is the white house, and they moved down there from Clinton County, where he first started by giving all his weekly pay checks to the local telegraph operator; and when he saw how much better it would be in Cincinnati they moved out of the little town where he was born so that he could more easily go across the river into the gambling houses in Kentucky to begin his play each evening.

He had his lunch box and the four dollars he got for pawning her fox fur again so he was starting out even earlier tonight. He was just leaving as the truck pulled up. The driver said here is an electric refrigerator from the Syndicate.

The driver backed the truck up to the little porch: the orange moving van was about as large as the house. Under the bridge was the last of what had been a slum before the other houses gave away to cobblestone streets and the hunched abutments of warehouses. Now even the warehouse owners were cautious because Cincinnati so often floods; this little doll house was perched above the web of tracks and streets,

forgotten because it was under the raised part of the bridge
or maybe the house survived because it was small and no one
happened to think of demolition.

Maybrik looked at this new white refrigerator. The van
driver had removed the padded brown quilts: it was white
and inviolate in the lowering sun, like a block of ice. Maybrik
thought at once he could get one thousand dollars on it, maybe less, but with any amount he could maybe beat them with
their own present, and this pleased him.

"Oh no, I know it won't," the woman said. "I just know it
won't."

The driver squinted his old mover's eye.

"Lady, no need to feel bad. I've seen it before. Some of
these houses just weren't built for a beautiful icebox like this.
I wish we had one, but I don't think we ever will."

Maybrik stood to one side. In the first place he was sus-
picious. He could remember no raffle. But then he was often
drinking and troublesome in the Syndicate's places of business, so he wasn't always exactly certain what he had done;
but he did know he had a bad feeling about this refrigerator
in the house. Nothing they ever owned had been new when
they bought it.

"I'll leave it here," the driver said. "You get it inside the
best way you can. Maybe you will have to alter your front
door a little. Sign here."

The woman reached for the clip board and eagerly signed
her husband's name.

"How we going to run it?" Maybrik said when the orange
van had slipped away between the warehouses. "Isn't our
current still off?"

They both knew this was so.

"Tonight I was going to try for those back light bills," he
said. "Now I don't know."

The woman looked at the refrigerator on her porch and
at their narrow door. She ran into the house, crying. But she
did not cry too loudly because both children were in the
first minutes of sleep.

The haze of coal smoke from the shanty boats and the mauve and green running lights of the tugs and barges out on the river made it time for him to work.

Maybrik walked quickly to the edge of the porch and began to climb a wooden ladder that led from the small house to the top of the bridge abutment. From this abutment, if he did not slip down and snag the sharp pieces of wire and steel set in the cement all the way down to the water, he could climb over the railing at the top. In ten minutes he would be inside a casino.

Maybrik walked across the bridge and he looked down the strong impenetrable surface of the river, stretching away to Louisville, Cairo, and finally to New Orleans. He saw himself wearing a needle-point vest, aboard a brightly lighted river boat, dealing Faro to the aristocrats. For the shanty boats and the people who lived by drifting and the seasonal rise and fall of the yellow gouging river, Maybrik had only contempt. He always spat over the rail as he treaded the high burning air of the Suspension Bridge above them.

He walked quickly toward that first moment when the dice would hit the green cloth, when he could lean forward to read their faces after the moment of tumbling. When he returned home he recaptured each sequence of bets for his wife, and the children too, if they were awake. In this way Maybrik kept her happy because he was nearly always too tired for anything else; besides this gave her delight enough.

She had married him because of something she had never tried to explain, even to herself. Of course she had been warned against him by the older women in the small town where they both grew up. Maybrik's father's bankruptcy was well known; their warnings were clear enough. First Miss Sears said he was devoted to sport—not a good thing for so young a man, but that he did have the most boyish face. Then Mrs. Maudie Walker said through the grill of the stamp window at the Post Office that he was sweet enough if you just ever knew where he was at nights. It was known he drove the country roads furiously, often with the headlights

turned off. There were other stories of his fast Willys-Over-
land leaving four skid marks on sharply breaking country
roads. But she remembered him most vividly when he was
younger. There was a machine at the railroad station that did
not always give a piece of gum for the penny. Maybrik, as a
pretty child, used to slip up to this gum machine and try with
the coin he had saved. When the machine refused to give him
the gum—about half the time—he would walk off with her
without saying a word. So Maybrik sold her car on their
honeymoon and lost the money at a place called The Rock,
just outside Saratoga. Often after that, when Maybrik wanted
to be nice to her, he would recall vividly the exact sequence
of the dice in that chuck-a-luck cage; she understood this
about him. Finally when the telegraph operator became
stricken by conscience, Maybrik and his new wife moved to
Cincinnati. Now he would go across the river at nights and
stay twenty or thirty hours. After that he would stay up and
pace the small kitchen. He would tell her each action, each
play, until he had described his final loss.

"Nine, the point was nine!" he would shout. "And I lost.
Lost. Oh, it's so damned hard."

"Well, maybe the games *are* crooked," she would say and
pour him some coffee.

"No. NO!" he would rage, for he could never consider
this. He battered his dice-throwing hand again on the wall.

All the next morning the two children would play quietly
in the little house because he was sleeping. Shortly after noon
he would have to go to the pawnshop or to establish credit
somewhere. He would bring home just enough food for her
and the children. He seldom ate, but he always carried the
lunch bucket. He considered his trip across the bridge his
work. At 6 P.M. each night he climbed his ladder and headed
for one of the Syndicate casinos.

He nodded to the keepers in the lighted toll booth near the
end of the bridge.

They let him pass because they knew he would simply
lower himself under the bridge again and go across under

their feet on the girders. The thought of him suspended under them and above the yellow consuming river, to save fifteen cents was too much for the tollkeepers. So they let him pass.

Maybrik, however, felt this was a legitimate earning and, in fact, argued on several occasions that he was entertain-. ment for them. Even when he spidered under the bridge all that first winter, he felt he did not steal his passage to Covington. Sometimes they leaned out of their toll booth and called, you are a character, and then Maybrik would stomp like a troll across the bridge and would not speak to them for at least two days.

At the Kentucky end of the bridge he turned left. The Syndicate owned all the places in Covington and even farther south. Maybrik had heard of gamblers on the Ohio side, in Cincinnati, but he could never find anyone who was a really independent professional. Sometimes, at the casinos, he thought he recognized a few men who were regulars but when the gambling started he was too busy for nonprofessional talk, or even to inquire from the houseman.

He was admitted into The Club. This one was called only The Club. The Syndicate's places had brown fronts for they bought their paint in industrial lots. All their neon signs out front said EAT, but there were only a few sandwiches and some old coffee, in case a stranger accidentally got in and really did want to eat. The Syndicate, in fact, controlled all of Covington and Maybrik sometimes felt the river was part of Covington right up to the Ohio bank. The Syndicate did not want to own the shanty boats *on* the river because they were leaky or they would slip away. The Syndicate did own the streetcar line, the elevators in all the buildings, the railroad station, the roller skating rink, and all the taxis. This was one reason Maybrik always walked even when he was winning a little. Also he intended to speak less to the toll bridge men for he felt the Syndicate also might have an interest in the bridge even now.

The white linen cloths were already being taken off the

dice tables. There were a few people standing around waiting for the houseman to hang up his coat and to roll his sleeves.

The houseman glanced at the end of the table where Maybrik stood in his usual place. Maybrik was short and stocky and his red hair was awry, and glowed under the droplight.

"That Man is back, huh?" the houseman said. "Well, we will see what they say tonight."

Maybrik and the houseman were almost friends. Their's was a kind of mutual respect, as men of two line battalions have for each other when they have been dug in opposite each other in one sector, all winter long. For it is then a man peeps through the sniper-scope and sees cross-haired that extra tall one who passes out the mail at noon; so you try to shoot the strangers on each side, and save the tall one until later. This standoff, Maybrik felt, was certainly very near to friendship.

This houseman, however, sometimes gave Maybrik advice, like "Lay Off" or "You are all right *to*night, Red." Once Maybrik was losing and the houseman gave him five dollars too much in change, but Maybrik could not say if this were error. He afterwards felt it was.

Maybrik cracked his knuckles and did not answer the houseman. This was a good night: he had the money from the fox fur again, and the pawnshop keeper, who was a kind of personal banker, had given him twenty-five dollars to invest. Without the pawnshop keeper, who kept so many of their possessions—the two suits, the books, the washing machine, the potted ferns—Maybrik knew they could not go on, so he was flattered by the pawnshop keeper's encouragement. In fact the pawnshop keeper recently mentioned a less strenuous job: clerking among the old magazines, the rusty musical instruments, the racks of old clothes that customers had left through the years. Maybrik at first detested the pawnshop keeper for this offer but in the past two weeks they had been cordial—no arguments about the worth of the fox fur, for example.

Maybrik threw two one-dollar bills on the table and held

the dice in the palm of his hand. In his left hand the rest of the money folded lengthwise between his fingers, making a crowned fist, the blossom of some very remarkable flower.

The dice dripped from his fingers and bounced in hot neurotic parabolas against the bang board: eleven.

"Let it ride,"

Maybrik snatched up the dice so quickly that his finger tips burned on the hard green cloth.

In only three hours the houseman told him, now come into the Manager's office.

Maybrik had not expected this so soon, but he had lost even the lunch bucket. The houseman had faded it without changing expression; not at its value, but with a hasty wad of bills thrown on the table. Now he motioned, come to the office.

"Now you look here," the manager of Number Three Club said and he leaped at Maybrik. "Now you look here!"

The manager was flushed.

Maybrik took the corner of the manager's table for a seat and hung his short legs over the side. On the desk he saw the twenty-five dollars, and his shoes.

"This here money," the manager said. "Stolen. It was marked. It's from our pawnshop across the river."

Maybrik did not answer. He was stunned. But he knew his feeling about the pawnshop and about the job offer had been right.

"He reported to us. And you have got possession."

Maybrik was not angry at his betrayal. He had known all along, really, that the pawnshop keeper had been too anxious to help.

Maybrik was only thinking about the house across the river and his wife.

"Furthermore," the manager said as he got to the point, "we don't want you hanging around here."

Maybrik was hurt. He had believed he was wanted simply because he was a man who followed his profession. It was as natural for him to gamble as it was for a train to run on its tracks.

"You are a nickel and dime person. You bring lunches. You cause trouble when you are drinking. It is the same in all our places. Why pick on Number Three? I'm sick of it."

Maybrick wriggled his toes. He felt it was better not to take issue on the trumped-up charges about the money. That, he felt, was simply their excuse. But it was one which could be legal and potent if he were accused officially.

"Your hunches and your system . . . gone far enough. You know we could have you on this pawnshop thing?"

Maybrik said he felt they could but he would promise not to play systems. He would even place larger bets if that was wanted.

The manager became red at the collar and then at the ears.

"Not the point! You're driving away business. People with the big stuff can't stand you around. You get it?"

Maybrik nodded. He wanted only to get home.

"Then we understand each other. We tried to be nice with that refrigerator. But that wouldn't do. Some guys don't learn."

"That's what I don't understand," Maybrik said. "I earned every cent from you people. What raffle?"

Then they threw the shoes at him and hustled him into one of their taxis which was waiting outside and took him across their toll bridge and let him out abruptly on the Cincinnati end. And they said, By God don't ever come back.

Then their taxi drove back across their bridge and did not stop at their toll booth.

Maybrik climbed slowly down his own wooden ladder to the porch of the small white house. It was two o'clock in the morning. The shanty boats were asleep in darkness, drifting and curtsying to each other on the broad unlighted river. His wife was still up.

"You forgot to bring home your lunch box, Honey."

Maybrik shook his head.

"And your shoes, too?"

He nodded. He had left them in the taxi, even though they had thrown the shoes at him.

"Well I am glad you are home early. Tell me about the first play."

She began to make the coffee. And so he told her.

". . . Except now I'm barred. For life. And there are no tables in Cincinnati where I can get bets down. Just none at all."

She nodded. "And I suppose they have the other pawn-shops?"

"Yes," he said. "I just didn't think it would be tonight. I suppose I ought to get a job. Maybe driving a cab."

She saw him clearly for a second, in a billed cap, cruising the lonely streets, maybe in winter, looking for passengers. She began to whimper a little and said no. Not ever have to do that.

Maybrik told her about the refrigerator.

"It's a kind of dividend for us. Sometimes the houseman wins a car, or a set of dishes, or some dancing lessons. They draw names out of a hat. They fixed this raffle. For me. They wanted to pay me off and they did it that way because they figured we needed a refrigerator, and they have too many. Besides, we spoiled business."

Maybrik was suddenly angry. He jumped up and yelled something. He slammed the door of the house.

Outside a light rain came drifting across the river. From the deck of one of the sleeping shanty boats he stole the large coil of rope. He carried the loose end up the wooden ladder and pulled it taut.

The first two cars he flagged on the bridge paid no attention. The third one stopped, but pulled away after he explained.

Then the Model A Ford stopped. It was full of working-men. They were drinking.

"Hey Ed," the driver called into the rear seat. "This guy wants to pull up a refrigerator."

The car seemed to split from one huge laugh.

They all got out to see. One of the men in overalls sat on the curb holding his sides and said Christ what a night, what a deal.

The man named Ed threw a bowline knot on the rear bumper and one of the others leaned over the rail and looked down.

"It's there, all right. I thought he was kidding."

"O. K., try it in low gear," Ed called and he stood near the railing of the bridge with his hand in the air for "Go Ahead."

The car had pulled ahead slowly on the wet pavement. Ed motioned "Stop."

All seven of them lifted the white refrigerator over the railing and set it on the sidewalk and then stood around it laughing.

"Just lift it up on the back bumper," Maybrik said. "We'll take it out in the middle."

The man on the curb couldn't get up. He kept holding his sides and saying, he won it in a raffle. So it won't go in the door. And he ain't got no shoes, Oh Christ what a night what a deal.

They perched the new white refrigerator on the rail of the bridge above the middle of the swollen river. Maybrik held it steady with one hand.

"Now let her ride," he said.

Ed kicked the back panel.

The white refrigerator fell end over end. The door flew open just as it hit. The top flew off and floated like a small white duck for a second, and then slid beneath the cold water.

"Good job," Maybrik said. "Thanks a lot."

The drunken workmen were still laughing in the rain. The one man got up from the curb but he was still holding his sides. What a night. He ain't got no shoes at all. What a deal.

"It's all right," the driver said from the window of his car after they were all loaded. "We will run into you again sometime."

And then they drove laughing past the lighted box where the tollkeepers were dozing.

Down in the little house Maybrik was going to tell about the workmen who had piled out of their car and had helped him. But his wife was crying.

"We couldn't have kept it," Maybrik told her. "The landlord would have taken it for the rent. Maybe the Syndicate already has an interest in this side of the river. In that case the box still belonged to them anyway."

His wife did not answer. Someone was knocking at the front door.

Maybrik opened it.

The man outside said he had a car so come on.

He had been looking for the address since the houseman gave him Maybrik's name. Outside the motor of the car was still running and the headlights showed the rain was coming down in earnest.

The wife carried the little girl and Maybrik took the sleeping boy toward the stranger's car. Suddenly Maybrik realized there was nothing left in their home: no clothes, no furniture, no washing machine, no potted ferns. There were only the scraps of the last food he had brought home.

It was raining harder and he looked back under the bridge at their gutted empty house. Then, from habit, he left the car a second and went back and locked the door. He turned and threw the key toward the shanty boats sleeping in the river.

As they drove between the warehouses the man with the car talked softly because of the children.

"The rest of us were kicked out tonight, too. I was cleaned out at their Number Six and my acquaintance got the same thing at their Number Twelve, the Club on East Fifth. We are finished, I think."

Maybrik nodded. Now he was glad about the refrigerator, as though he had preserved an integrity he had to test each day.

"We have a group," the driver said. "Up on Price Hill. There are seven of us now. It will make a nice little game. Faro."

Maybrik was excited about the prospect and he nodded eagerly.

"All our families can live in separate rooms, under our own casino in the attic. See?"

Maybrik was happy. He would miss the light and the noise and the houseman; he would miss even more the people who sometimes gathered around to watch him lose. But this large house up on Price Hill would be fine.

He looked down into the face of his sleeping boy.

"I swear," he told his new great friend, the driver. "If he ever looks at a card I'll beat him. It's not worth it."

"Now don't you dare say that when he can hear you," his wife said from the back seat.

And behind him for the first time Maybrik missed the steady presence of the river.

Through the threshing windshield wiper Maybrik looked ahead, thinking already about the nice days when he would slip back down to the Suspension Bridge and stare into the yellow water of the river, from above.

Up in the Yards

Up in the Yards

The next day I was being drafted, so in the way of a very young man, I walked out my mother's back door and across a meadow where once I flew kites, to the railroad siding. Perhaps this was a way of viewing my own past, before I moved on: from civilian to soldier, from boy to man. I felt it was one final walk across the landscape of my youth.

The right of way was a slash of industry across the warm, flat countryside. The section gang's tool shed still squatted beside the empty cattle pens; the creosote was black and glistened on a pile of crossties. West of town the rails spread outward into a broad delta of ballast rock and switch frogs and lonely, empty freight cars. At the end of the yards, a mile away, the tracks singled up once more and finally became a single glint of light on the horizon. At noon the yards were without noise, except beyond the right of way the engine of a tractor grew louder, then faded. Spring. Somewhere a farmer was plowing.

I could not believe it: in the yards, on the same crosstie, at the identical switch, I saw a wad of black, greasy waste, the kind that is packed around the axle of a freight car. Perhaps you have seen this packing on fire, or smoking, as you waited at a crossing for a slow train to pass.

I saw the greasy waste and at the identical moment I heard a faint *scruump*, the noise of many clubs, or gun butts, dropping to the ground. This small noise was only an engine being turned off inside a feed mill, far down the tracks. But the piece of waste lying in the sun, and the noise of a turned-off engine brought back that afternoon and that night.

I was ten years old. The hot sun of June rumbled like a freight train overhead. Winter had melted into ponds or had flowed down the creeks, or was held, still, in the leaf-rotted pools in Simpkin Woods. There must have been a few pools in the deeper woods because the frogs croaked in their old primitive way, calling boys into the swamps.

I was "helping" my father, for one of our fields joined the railroad's land, near a siding.

"Well, you have done good," my father said at the end of a row, for he noticed I was beginning to play.

"That so?" I said, and tried to sound something like him when he was given a compliment. In the country a boy learns to turn praise away, lest it appear a boast.

My father smiled, "Hell-yes, you done good," and then added, "Go on over there, if you want to." He was the best-hearted man in the world.

As I climbed over the fence to railroad property he called, "Watch out for trains."

I was going to boil a potato. I had one saved out in each pocket, and cattle salt in an empty tobacco tin.

To boil a potato up in the yards was more than simply wasting time. I think my father—who was a hunter while he lived—understood the savage appeal of fire to a boy. Or perhaps to start your own fire was to pretend, briefly, to manhood. To ride a freight train, alone, might come later, but now all I wanted was fire, and to cook food under the sky.

At a dump, where people from Sedley carted their refuse, I

found an enameled store sign: Pay Car Tobacco. There was a clean half-gallon tin, and settled water in the ditch.

With the sign, I scooped a hole the size of a small dog from the bank along the siding. The sign over the hole made a furnace; in the gravel bank was an opening for a smoke hole. Not far away a refrigerator car was empty, its doors open. Inside a reefer there is always wood.

On the same car, I opened the little door on the axle housing and took out the black, greasy waste. In a minute the black smoke poured upward from the dog-hole furnace, and I was staring into the core of a fire where pieces of lath writhed in the flames. The water in the can boiled. Suddenly I was hungry.

The world beyond the lovely, industrial hum of the telegraph poles, and the encircling woods, all those places I had not yet traveled, came into my daydreams; yet I also heard the steady *caarp-caaarp* of the frogs calling through the scrub oak, sumac, and the rustling pawpaw trees.

I thought—at first—a dog jumped from the refrigerator car. But it was the man's olive-drab blanket roll. The blanket roll leaped from the boxcar door, then lay flat and lifeless beside a crosstie.

The man himself was a shadow in the shadows of the reefer car, but he was so incredibly tall he seemed to fill the whole door. He thrust his head out of the darkness and I saw his face. In the sunlight his whiskers seemed on fire. He turned his face each way in the sunshine, and then seemed to calculate the distance to the main crossing in Sedley, a half mile below the yards. The man spat toward his own blanket roll, then jumped, stiff-legged, to the gravel. I did not want to think he noticed me, but he did. He looked once at the sky, and then at me. We were alone. I thought of all the rabbits I had surprised in a certain fence corner not far away.

As he came closer his shoes sent small rocks flying. His shoes, which had steel safety caps on the toes, came close to my fire, and stopped. Only then did I look up.

The man was dressed in wool, the kind soldiers wear: olive-drab shirt, a belt of old harness leather, olive-drab trousers. On his head was a square, black, quilted cap, with a tiny visor, the kind a fireman on a steam pile driver might wear.

"You woke me up," he said. "When you made them lath."

The inside of the refrigerator car had been dark.

"Don't you know that's stealing?"

"That so?" was all I could say, and I would have made a run for it except the man in the old army clothes began to laugh. That is, he raised his head and showed his flat, chipped teeth.

"Take all you can get off'num," he said. "Elst they will take it off of you."

Without saying anything else the man squatted down before my dog-hole furnace and held his hands toward the fire. This seemed to make us in league, bonded by our past, common crimes. The fire felt good on the tips of his fingers. The potato skins were already cracking in the steam.

A knife appeared in his hand. The blade snapped open. The blade was thin, and leather-stropped. All day he must have whetted the blade on his own shoe leather while he rode the freights. With a quick stabbing motion above the fire, he caught one of the potatoes on his knife.

"Our spuds is about done."

"You take them," I said. "I was . . . fooling around."

"Fool around while you can, elst they . . ." He looked down the rails toward town, as though he expected to see someone coming along the right of way. He rubbed the back of his hand across his lips.

He laid both potatoes on the overhanging edge of the sign, and cut them into six even parts. Almost delicately he speared one slice, and when the steam was gone he touched the potato to my pile of cattle salt. Then he ate.

"I've et worse for breakfast," he said. "And Kid, so will you."

"Wheeling," he said when I finally asked him. "Wheeling, West Virginia. Sister there."

"These clothes? Why you might say I collected them, for this little trip to Wheeling."

I had asked him because the old army clothes made me think he might have been Over There, a doughboy in France, had fought The Hun. Memorial Day was just past, and the Drum and Bugle Corps had marched to the cemetery. All of that was fresh in my mind.

Suddenly, above us on the bank, above my dog-hole furnace, I saw Foskett.

Foskett was the railroad's detective, for this Division. He lived in Sedley, with his wife. No children. If there was trouble anywhere along the line, Foskett had to investigate. They say Foskett once shot a car robber near Oakley, but even when there was a depression, when there were so many men on the road, they say Foskett never threw a man off a moving train. He did not carry a blackjack. The gun, however, was always in his shoulder holster, a 38 Special, well known. Foskett had been up in our yards, and I had not seen him walking toward the fire between the two cuts of cars.

Foskett stood on the bank, looking down. I noticed his hair was parted on the extreme right, and was the glistening black of creosote on new crossties. He worked in a faded blue denim jacket, and except for the holster, Foskett looked much like an ordinary brakeman.

"You boys eating a bite?" Foskett said, and he looked closely at the man who squatted beside my fire.

The man did not look up, but he stabbed at three more chunks of potato, as though to harvest them quickly.

"Yes, you are," Foskett said. "You are eating a bite. I saw that black greasy smoke from down the way.

"Would you have took some car packing to start your fire, Billy?"

He was talking to me.

At first I thought he was pretending he did not know me or my father and all of my relatives. I liked being called "you boys" as though I were also on the road. But it was the first time The Law ever addressed me.

The man in olive drab stood up.

"My fire," the man said. "The kid had potatoes, and I had me a fire. Like you said, just eating a bite."

Foskett looked off in the direction of our field. Perhaps from the bank he could see my father working.

"Would I have seen you on Number Twelve, at Urbancrest?"

The man did not answer. He began to kick gravel into the embers of the fire. I stood up also. The man seemed even larger as he threshed his shoes in the ballast, kicking even larger rocks into the hole. His face did not change expression, but he was leaving.

"Oh, finish your bite to eat," Foskett told the man, and then Foskett made a gesture with his thumb toward the fence that divided railroad property from the farms beyond. Foskett's thumb was an order for the man to move on.

Foskett turned to walk down through the yards toward town. But he stopped to call back, "Billy, your dad is looking for you."

I turned and ran.

My father was still at work in our two-acre patch, not far from the railroad.

"Back in the same day," my father said, as I climbed over the fence to his side. I felt better.

I took my hoe and began working along an open furrow. My father believed a good crop came from earth that was already warm. He always held off planting until after Memorial Day—considered too late, by some. He always put the eyes in the potato chunks facing the sky. This, however, was only superstition. Of all the potato growers around Sedley, my father was one of the best.

As I worked I kept remembering my fire. The man had said it was his fire, started with greasy waste, when it was not. Yet there was no reason to lie, because Foskett knew me and my father.

When I got to the end of the row, my father was standing

beside the fence. He was listening to the man in old army woolens.

The man had followed me. Now I was near my father and I thought the man had come because he had some claim.

"Well," my father said to the man, "will you work?"

The man threw the blanket roll across the fence to our side. He showed his flat chipped teeth and said, "I'll work."

The man balanced himself on the fence, and then crashed into the brush on our side. My father therefore knew the man was not from the country, and never had been.

"Take Billy's hoe for a couple of hours. He's just put in one hullva day. Up since daylight."

This was my father's good-natured way of letting me go home during the heat of the afternoon. He did not like to see his only son working all day, too soon. Life, he always said, was too short for that.

The man ignored me. He picked up my hoe and then, impulsively, chopped into the warm, dry soil. He pulled the black loam over the eyes of a potato chunk—then back—then tamped it with a surprisingly gentle tap of the hoe.

"Is that it?" he asked, and looked at my father, as though there were a secret, as though the soil would suddenly let out a chime of music, from below the surface, if everything were done just so.

Father nodded, "Just go on to the next one."

Quickly, even delicately, the man covered a half dozen more hills.

He was already sweating through the army woolens, so he came back to his bedroll to strip. Underneath the woolen shirt was another shirt of faded blue denim, something like Foskett's faded jacket.

"I like this," he said and showed his flat teeth which were chipped all the way back into his mouth—from opening bottles with his teeth.

"I wouldn't mind at all, doing this."

Then he and my father turned. Each in a row, they worked to the far end of the field. This was only a patch, the point rows of a back field, but it was real potato land: well-drained loam that broke up almost like ashes. At the far end the two men turned and came back; as a matter of courtesy my father let the new man lead out at his own pace. Back and forth they swung, in easy unison, their hoes making a *chuk-chuk* as they covered the rows which were straight as gun barrels.

At the end of fifty minutes, my father stopped. This was courtesy to a new man, to let him blow and get his second wind.

"Jesus, I wouldn't mind doing this *all* the time," the man said again, and began to take off his denim shirt. Underneath was his underwear, surprisingly white, of summer weight. In the sun, his skin was almost transparent as though he had never before been exposed to light. The man held his arms out straight and looked at the black ring near his wrists, where his hands began.

". . . If I was able, I would like it all the time. If I was steady."

My father looked across the right of way, toward the yards. It was not customary to inquire at once about a man's past, nor about his immediate health, unless there was something anyone must notice: an arm in a sling, or a pair of crutches. Therefore my father remained silent. If a man said he was not a steady worker, it could mean anything. But to me, just after Memorial Day, it could mean only one thing. War.

From the little den I had hollowed out of the brush of the fence row, I said:

"Were you in the War? At the Front?"

The man dropped his hoe, and stamped one huge, steel-capped shoe down into the furrow. Suddenly, in a spasm of anger, he seemed to shake hands with himself. He took one step down the row he had just covered, and stamped his foot again, as though to drive the buried potato chunk into the center of the earth.

"Bell-ow Woods," he told my father, who had not moved.

"And Cap'n, they ordered us to attack, and then they opened up on us from a hill . . ."

"Yes," my father said, and hesitated to say more. When the man turned, my father saw a number stenciled plainly across the back of the undershirt.

"Would they have let you out of the Vets' Hospital, up the line?"

The man calmed down at once. He picked up the hoe, and looked down along another furrow. He knew my father was goodhearted for he said, "Yes. You might say they let me go."

"But I went through it all," the man added. "And last night they kicked me off a freight. A brakeman done it."

He looked across the yards, and swore.

"Billy," my father said as he turned to his next row, "your mother is looking for you."

As I walked past the huge man, he took off his fireman's cap. From behind the cap, I heard him say very softly, "Never get in bad, Kid."

The quilted cap covered up the sounds, but I had not thought his hair could be so gray.

My father got home earlier than usual.

Together they had finished out the point rows. After the last row the man had put on his two shirts, and my father had given him wages, and a dollar extra.

That was the spring my father allowed me to ride a bicycle after dark. To ride at night was something like climbing the fence to the right of way. While Father listened to the early news, and while Mother was in the kitchen; I pedaled into the evening, hearing, still, my father's voice as I left, ". . . Watch out for automobiles."

By nine I had pedaled the back roads, past Simpkin Woods, where gravel hissed in the darkness under the bicycle wheels. At the crossing in town there was a crowd under a street light.

"I got the necktie," a boy said. He was holding up a four-in-hand, under the street light. The knot was sliced in two.

The ends of the tie might fit around a man's neck, except the knot was slashed.

"Foskett dropped it. He made it to the restaurant, and dropped his necktie."

Up in the yards, where once you saw the green and red and amber switch lights, or the moonbeams adrift on the rails, I saw their flashlights. Two dozen beams tracked in the darkness. First on the ground, then whetting against one another as they pointed toward the clouds. The men already had gone into the yards. The flashlights were pointing under, then on top of the boxcars along the siding.

For the first time I noticed all the people under the street light, drawing back from the slashed necktie, all of them boys. Some my age; some nearly grown.

The flashlights in the yards converged on the ground, all on one spot.

"They got him," said the boy who had picked up Foskett's tie. "We better go see it."

I went, too, stumbling over the rails in the darkness. The boys talked as we stumbled along . . .

". . . He got more wine, and was walking up and down. A rock in his hand . . ."

"He asked the Bailey girl did she want to go up in the woods. To have her picture taken . . ."

In the yards, the circle of men with flashlights was gathered around a switch tie. They carried a flashlight in one hand, a shotgun or a club in the other.

The circle drew closer. I pushed, and was pushed from behind. I entered the middle of the circle of light on the ground.

First I saw the blanket roll. Then I saw the black, quilted cap. In the center of the wool shirt I saw the hopeless, cold brown splotches. Bullet holes. The face was staring upward into the hard, low clouds.

Near the hand, where the knife lay, above his head, was a piece of dark greasy waste. Someone had dropped it there during the winter. A clot of waste on the end of a switch tie.

Their flashlights went out. There was the sudden silence of

a man's held breath in the darkness. Then, faintly, *scruuump:* together the men dropped their gun butts and clubs to the gravel.

The next day my father took it on himself to find the next of kin, but no one ever did come from Wheeling, West Virginia. We found out the man bought the wine with what he earned, and then spent the extra dollar on rubbing alcohol. Foskett met him again in the yards and was about to tell him once more to get off the right of way.

"No, Billy," my father said. "The dollar beyond wages didn't likely make the difference. He brought it on himself. If you saw Foskett's neck, you know he had to do it. The necktie knot saved Foskett's jugular."

When I asked if the man really was an old soldier and had been Over There, my father said he did not really know. "But he was a veteran, Billy. Or they wouldn't have kept him at the Vets' Hospital. Up the line."

. . . A wad of black, greasy waste on a switch tie. A turned-off engine, and the silence, except for a tractor plowing, which first seemed far away, then near . . .

Within two years, my father died, of natural causes. When the war in Europe came on my mother sold the farm and we moved to a smaller house in Sedley, not far from the railroad. As my father was too young for the First War, so was I too young for Korea by three months. Now it was my turn to go in the peacetime draft, and I wanted to get it over.

So I thought I never again would hear the noise of clubs or gun butts dropping to the ground, almost at the same time, but I did.

When a training battalion is assembled in the center of an infantry camp, in Texas, and when you have been on the firing range all day, and when the entire battalion stands too long at present arms, you hear that identical noise, the noise of hands slapping the taut slings of rifles, hundreds of hands slapping taut leather almost at the same instant, for order arms, when the sun is going down.

That identical noise, except fainter, and the hopeless

splotch of waste on a switch tie brought more than a memory. As I turned back to my mother's house, I suddenly knew I would ask the first nice girl—even if she was not entirely pretty, but if she was nice—I would ask her to marry me. I would ask her against the day when the world was a freight yard.

And that is what happened.

I met my sergeant's daughter one evening in Texas, after the sun went down. We were standing on her porch, and love is what I called it, and after a minute she said, yes. Yes. Through the window I saw the half-averted profile of her father. The sergeant from habit was erect in his customary chair, his khaki shirt still pressed, glittering from starch in the bright parade ground light inside the room. His profile was someone I remembered—of Foskett, yes, and my father too. But, for the moment he was looking the other way, and so I kissed her.

Under the Boughs
of Ambition

Under the Boughs
of Ambition

Elethy was sick, but when he promised to come home directly from Survey, she got up and ate a bite and kissed him good-by, good-by, at their front door.

The chain grinding around and around the bicycle's sprocket was what he heard as he sighted down the long ski-jump hill, aiming himself at the campus below. Bent forward over the handle bars, the books in the humped cloth pouch on his back, the cap reversed to give the slant of great speed, he pedaled furiously through a stop sign.

The driver of the milk truck honked, dropped clip board and pencil, stomped brake, curbed it. Going to get it yet, was what the driver would be saying, though each morning at 8:50, the cap bill turned backwards above the handle bars ran the same intersection dangerously because everyone in town knew he was old and mighty active and absent-minded, y'see?

At the fire station, he pulled the chain of his siren whistle. (He had told Elethy he needed the siren for dogs.) A city fireman tilted on a chair behind glass lifted his fat pinochle face and waved in sleep at the green satchel disappearing across the windowpane. In the street behind, the milk truck scuttled like a big white bug across the street.

Secretly he knew he was a great teacher, a real inspiration. Year after year, the avalanche of semesters buried some of the younger teachers, but he had the gift for it. When a class got up at the end of that final hour of that final day in the ghostly precision of a class breaking up, never to meet again, he always called from the lectern, "Ah, much have we traveled in the realms of gold . . ." And then he hastened to sit in absolute judgment on every examination paper.

Inside the stone gates of the campus he ran one final red light. He threw the bicycle carelessly—publicly—on the English Department shrubbery. Two minutes late he walked into Romantic Survey classroom.

Usually, he managed to arrive two minutes late and to enter lecturing. Now, mouth open, he stood at the door. He faced the larger maw of an empty classroom where oak and black iron desks were like rows of brown serrated teeth.

Someone had done it again. The sign was still on the blackboard: No Survey Today, per John Clare.

Sometimes these obscene little notices on the blackboards were signed Coleridge. But the name John Clare shook him, for who in class would know a minor figure, insane toward the end, at that?

But the classroom was before him. He could sense the warm rustle of lately departed students; he could distinctly smell the purple of forbidden cigarette smoke. He looked across each row, as though his glasses were at fault. He wanted to see some of the English majors, with their notebooks open. There were none. No loyalty any more, he thought. None.

With one raging foot he mounted the platform. Would lecture anyway. It was the stuff of legend, like his racing bike, and the public, early morning scoot down the hill. Just let that get around: Old Henry carrying on the good work, to an empty room.

He dumped the green cloth satchel of books across the table, and dropped on it the one book, especially bound, he carried to throw at someone knitting or smoking or, in the back rows after a big dance night, sleeping. He cleared his throat at the empty room. For a second he hesitated, threw back the lock of silver hair that roved his forehead. Tossing his mane, he knew the students called it. The open shirt collar, the white tennis sneakers, the lock of hair were all badges of his assertion; yet they seemed to fail him at this moment. He could not open his dry old throat.

As he put the folder of notes back into the satchel, a girl blundered through the door. Her knitting bag tangled in the door jamb. Her hair was combed only a little. Her eyes followed the narrow track of her own embarrassment upon the floor. Without raising her head, she tried to slip into her seat without her usual noise.

Miss Handschin was late again.

Always before he had saved his rebuke until Miss Handschin was thoroughly seated, until she hoped she was safe. Then he told her off. The class had come to expect it.

Now he suddenly realized that she was one of the faithful: late, perhaps, but always there. For this he loved her.

"Miss Handschin," he said without the usual gruffness which she had come to know so well at least twice each week.

She looked up from her scattered books, from the bag of knitting that sat at her feet like a leather puppy. For the first time she noticed they were alone. She started to get up. Then she sat down abruptly. Her face did not change expression; her eyes were still sleepy in the unlined round circle of her face.

"I—ah," he said. "I mean. Apparently we are not to pursue the muse this hour, Miss Handschin?"

It came to him they might have a class after all. The two of them. Intimate. The way every class should be, with Master and Pupil face to face. He would talk directly to her in the center of the classroom, beneath the purr of the fluorescent lights. And she would say, "Tell me, what *does* 'A sensitive plant in a garden grew,' whatever *does* it mean?"

And he would tell her, of course. Shelley and the Greats, and the rest of it. . . .

He could not, however, order her to stay in the vacant room. He could only say firmly, as he began to take the notes back out of the green satchel, "Now should we, Miss Handschin?"

For the first time she read the whole blackboard. The little notice was still chalk-white, blinking a little at her: per John Clare.

She giggled. Her foot kicked at her squat knitting bag.

"Oh, *I* thought . . ."

For a moment she did not move. She looked around for the others. The seats, in vacant tiers above and behind, were too much for her. Too often he had let her get firmly seated before he said what the class had come to expect. She stacked the purple anthology on top of her notebook. Without hesitation she grabbed the knitting bag by its leash.

"*I* thought it was the wrong day. Or something."

Then Miss Handschin bumped her way slowly down the long row of seats to the exit nearest the campus restaurant. There was the urgency of coffee in her disorder. She did not at all look back.

The knitting bag caught for a second on the door jamb. The pleats of her skirt switched once around the door, and Miss Handschin was gone.

Per John Clare. Though he erased the spot twice, the obscene little notice still blinked at him. And which student knew so much about John Clare, before the Greats?

Ellias: it came to him as he swept the eraser again and again over the blackboard. That little gadfly. Ellias with his Letters to the *Guard* on all subjects. Ellias who had brought suit in court for a refund on an English Department course he felt was inadequate. Had cited where the Professor lifted the lecture notes, word for word. The administration quashed it, but hadn't the newspapers around the state taken up that one?

Ellias, who on Monday said distinctly from the back of the room: "Dr. Aspel, don't you connect psychoanalysis with the *self*-analysis of the Romantic Mind, in general?"

"No, I don't," he had shouted back in his well-known irascible tone; the Old Lion roaring, the students said.

So he took off on "Sigh-cology" in general, and that was that.

Now Ellias was having his little revenge. Well, there were ways to handle that type. Even if Ellias were a senior and would want very much to graduate in a month. . . . Well, wanted to see Schaffeur anyway. So he erased the sign once and for all and put on the old plaid cap, the bill forward, and walked tantrum-like out of his empty classroom.

Outside, the day was bright. Spring was weaving strands of sunlight through the vines across all the windows of the English Department. At this hour, between classes, a few orange or blue jackets winked among the trunks of the tall firs, whose tops combed the higher breezes. Somewhere beyond the edge of the campus, up a valley, the final snows of winter would be melting into water; somewhere to the west across other, lower mountains were the chaste waves, the up-rearing shoulders of the Pacific.

He walked up steps and between pillars to Administration, to the Dean's office. The receptionist, as usual, guarded the doors.

Yes, had to see Dean Schaffeur at once. Yes, faculty business. And wasn't it the faculty that ran the school?

It seemed there was a meeting. Busy days in spring, you know. But could he wait?

He sat on the long hard oak bench in the outer office, drumming his fingers, or turning the plaid cap over and over, thinking how much the walls of marble resembled the interior of a savings bank. Administrators, they were, but he had learned to deal with them. He had heard it thunder more than once, over the years; he knew them all: Escroe and Schaffeur and . . .

Fair seed time had my soul, et cetera. So he had come to McVale College. In those days it was your Latin and Greek that meant something. He'd learned those from his mother, of course, very early. He was McVale's first man with a Ph.D. in the Romantic field; the first years he taught the whole of the *Prelude*, but later it was *Michael* he knew that students like the best. Finally they gave him the Romantic Survey: Order and Revolt in Poetry. Now every English major had to take it. And that was that.

Surely his fifth year at McVale was the one: by then all of his articles had come back from all of the journals for large, impossible corrections. He was no scholar. His old friends from the East did not ask him to speak, even after hints, at the Language Meetings. So he took his stand on teaching, he got his lecture notes in order for once and for all. But not dull. You could always change the order of things, from year to year.

With tenure, he could afford revolt, and so he did. First, they took him off the Planning Committee and then the Lectures Committee, and gradually he was totally free to teach. When Dr. Burns passed away, some dean wanted this Escroe for English Department Chairman. He revolted; held out for his own promotion; but, in time, he came out solidly for Escroe. And that was that.

In his full teaching maturity, of course, he rethought the Survey. He saw the weaknesses of all the Romantics. He became an image breaker. . . . Each year, in True Justice it had to be said Shelley was flat, insipid; then Byron's morality, he who went to a tavern in Spain to *have* his favorite barmaid before going through Customs. Coleridge, confused by the Germans; Keats's "Lamia," his *snake* woman. Keats the sniveler, that red-haired whining little man. But each year, by way of conclusion, he said, "After Keats, poetry died. And aesthetics took over." Had it come to this: an Ellias, an empty classroom, per John Clare?

The door swung open.

From the Dean's office, under purple clouds of smoke, the Department Heads, all in a row, wound past the long oak bench. Each Department Head glanced down and said in a smiling public way, "Why, hello *there*."

Escroe was last. Clearly, with his rolling administrator's eye, Escroe saw *someone* was going over his head to the Dean. He passed the bench with only a crisp nod of his head, cleared his throat for no reason at all.

"Now, Henry," the Dean said, after he had offered a cigarette and had withdrawn it quickly when he remembered how it was about smoking. But he added, "Now what's the problem . . . ah, this fine spring morning?"

Dean Schaffeur was all business. His forehead had the identical shine of the marble wainscoting around the office. It had been a good year for him, and with spring on the campus he was set to ride things out until graduation.

So he told Dean Schaffeur about "the larger issues of a University, the things too often overlooked in the scramble. For instance, the decay of personal discipline," and about "the Student Mind, and all these new trick courses. No Latin; no Greek. Frankly discouraging. Now this morning . . ."

"Yes?" Dean Schaffeur said, waiting like an official of a small loan office for an embarrassed customer to say exactly how much was needed. The Dean smiled a little. Escroe told him nearly everything. Those notices on the blackboard weren't good, but the students needed to have their jokes.

The older man hesitated, started to get up, then sat down abruptly. The door seemed far away.

"You know we depend on you older men," Schaffeur told him; this was at least half true.

"Yes. Yes, I *know* that."

"Just now the Department Heads discussed the Wardner

Prize. They decided on a student of yours . . . er, he's in your Survey. Your influence, of course."

For no reason at all he thought of Miss Handschin and her bag of knitting; he wondered if the knitting inside was like the uncombed hair on her head.

The electric clock on the wall behind the Dean did not purr, and yet the time leaked through the hammered brass shield. The sweep second hand crossed the minute and the hour hands in that interminable combat which becomes the years.

"We all felt he had breadth, Henry. That's certainly your criterion. Ellias is a smart boy."

He saw it. He remembered Escroe's rolling administrator's eye. They were all conspirators; they had walked in a line out of this office, cigarette smoke and all. No doubt Escroe pushed for Ellias; the others went along. And now. He recovered quickly. Too quickly.

"I'm here against that Communications course, Dean. I came about that. Last night I made up my mind. Why, it would lower standards. Why, why, I'd resign."

"Now, Henry," the Dean said easily as though he were humoring someone's mother. "We depend on you older men, y'know. Fact, Professor Escroe recommends we use your man Barnes. And it was thought . . ."

"But Communicate what?"

"Why, what we are, Henry. What we really are."

"Then I'll still . . ."

The tiers of empty seats came before his eyes. The notice on the blackboard. And now Ellias. . . .

"Yes?"

"Well, I'm on the record," he said with decision. "I wanted my feelings on the record."

The Dean was already letting him out the door.

"Drop in any time, Henry. I really do value getting you on the record. Give me a Memo on it. . . ."

The door closed behind him. He walked down the steps between fluted pillars.

At the bottom of the steps he looked out across the campus. The mauve and blue jackets, and girls in their first spring dresses flashed among the trunks of the fir trees. Well, in two more years he and Elethy would pull out; go to Florida. Retire. Fish it out. In Florida he would dress exactly like the tourists, and he would never have to protest anything again. Maybe there would be a secret little apartment somewhere, reserved to give expression to the Private Self, which he felt every man owed to himself, in the end.

He walked past the English Department shrubbery. He saw someone had parked his racing bicycle.

Classes were changing and the halls were crowded.

There was no mail in his box. After a seminar he would be finished for the day. Only the long afternoon and the long night remained.

In the outer office, the secretary permitted him to use the English Department telephone. He dialed home, dialed the top of the ski-jump hill. He waited impatiently for her to get out of bed. He knew Elethy was not really sick; only pretending. Then he talked loudly, so that Escroe, in his private office, could plainly hear.

"No, my love," he said. "Not home for lunch today. *All tied up*. No, not until *very* late this evening, Elethy, my love. Schaffeur's in trouble. Wants a Memo."

After Elethy hung up, he stood there for a single moment as though he were listening, perhaps to the words of love. But only the line whispered in his ear.

Inside a Budding Grove

Inside a Budding Grove

23 Suddley Avenue

Professor Gilbert Hannel Puce
Department of English
Prankins College, U of P
New Haven, Conn.

Dear Tuffy:

This time of year, as "The Bard" says, finds me with choirs aplenty but—alas—too few sweet birds. I envy you the brilliant autumn "back East" and I wish I could share it with you.

But to the problem: my son, Thomas Stearns, is now entering the Senior year of what, out here, we call "High School." Essentially Tommy is a good kid, of course, but he doesn't exactly take after his Old Man in ways which Merle and myself most approve. Had any problem like that with your Suzy?

Anyway, Tommy always holed up in our basement during our regular music hours. He always showed a real flair for things mechanical. Why he has had engines and white rats in the basement since he was a child, and he used to "operate" on the rats, playing Science, I guess. Now Tommy is six feet tall and weighs about two hundred. He got the motorcycle before I knew about it, but of course I was glad to find out

71

he was rebuilding that old automobile. I admit it: the damned thing runs. As to intellect, Tommy did start out as a "slow reader" but Merle kept after him and now he has read all through Shakespeare and Chaucer and those boys, and likes 'em.

Now: in looking through your catalogue, Tuffy, I notice there are some tuition scholarships. I wonder if these are sometimes awarded on a basis of geographical distribution? Also, which men in your department serve on the Selection Committee?

Naturally Tommy is set on being an English major, though I daresay you might not find him quite up to snuff—with *your* standards—for your "Advanced Crit. Intro"—still, T. S. might make a good student, later.

If Tommy knocks off one of your tuition things, Merle and myself could very well spend next year in Italy. I'd like to get at the project that Guggenheim turned down again. In Italy I'd really dig into Castelvetro. *There* was a Critic.

My best to your "gode wif" and all of yours. Glad to hear, indirectly, that your Suzy got married. Who was it?

Oh yes, if you hear of a Department that needs a Middle-English man, let me know. I find California very d-u-l-l.

Yep, still hear from Turnball: no like him.

> Yr Obedient Ser,
> Calvin Farkesgill
> Associate Professor, English

----

                                              23 Suddley Avenue
Professor Graecae Hannibal Turnball
Department of Classics
Templeton University
Huget, Georgia

Dear Hann:

This time of year finds me with all Gaul still divided—alas —and life continues its irregular paradigm. I envy you the brilliant autumn which you always enjoy in the South and I wish I could share it with you.

Tommy [Thomas Stearns, whom you will remember from the delightful year we spent on your campus—just old enough then to throw croquet balls at police cars] is now a big boy. Bigger than his old man: five-eleven and one ninety. Isn't your Clara a year younger? Anyway, Tommy is just finishing "High School" but I must say he never was passed through the early discipline which makes a classicist so very fine, like yourself—or a Middle-English man, for that matter.

An interesting mind, has Tommy. I mean not an outstanding mind, but an *interesting* one. He has a nice combination of energy and a real flair for putting things in their proper operating order. I haven't run him through the aptitude tests —don't need to—but Merle and I both think T. S. would make a swell linguist. God knows we need 'em, with Sputnik and all; otherwise what happens to the classics? Pretty much on his own he's been through Shakespeare and Chaucer. And of course he has heard a lot of music around the house.

Now: I just happened to glance through Templeton's catalogue. What about those Bob Jones, Jr., Out-of-State grants? Do you sit with the committee, or anything like that? What I really want is for Tommy to get some real discipline, and to live in a *cultured* community. Don't worry about him and segregation. He knows all about *that* . . . been through it with the wet backs, out here.

Hann, if we could finesse the tuition at Templeton for Tommy, that would see Merle and myself in "Merrie England" and once there I could clean up my Arthurian puzzle and the Roman influence, for once and for all. ACLS, incidentally, didn't see eye-to-eye with us about that grant . . . going to try a Rockefeller next.

My best to your "*Summmum Bonum.*" Say, wasn't that a dilly about Puce's daughter, Suzy? How long do you suppose that was going on? Merle says—ha ha—that's easy: just count on your fingers. The gent in the case, I hear, was Puce's

Graduate Assistant! Too bad about Scrutts's kid: flunked out of Cal Tec.

Was always sorry our visit back in '46 to your campus never came to anything, but I know you did your best. If you hear of an opening in Florida, let me know. Merle can't stand California weather. Also there isn't any Real classical activity in these parts.

Vale!
Cal Farkesgill
Associate Professor

---

23 Suddley Avenue

Professor J. D. Scrutts
Department of Anthropology
Galpar Tec., U of D
Scaddley, Wisconsin

Dear James Dudley:
This time of year finds our barrow rifled by the latter-day California Migrations, but our "culture" continues apace, and there are shards of pottery, etc., in every *arroyo*.

Actually, this note is in behalf of our sibling, Tommy. He's an entering Senior at San Salibar High. Perhaps you have heard of their "Pre-Science Junior Interne" program. Well, Thomas Stearns is right in the center of *that* and I tell you our basement, for years, has been full of arrowheads, camping stuff, etc. The kid has always been a real bug on the outdoors. Not that I blame him, of course, for this is wonderful country. Every week end T. S. heads out for the High Sierras, and he comes back with all sorts of interesting things. Lately he's been taking a girl along, and my they do have the best time.

Oh yes, reminds me: Clara Turnball (her mother is Hann's second wife) left Broadmore, and is now an airline stewardess. Also too bad about Puce's Suzy. Sins of the father, hey?

Well, anyway, I just happened to see Galpar Tec's catalogue, Jamie, and wonder if you had any information on the way they give the "Grant-in-Aid" things. I note they are for students of "high personal merit" and I believe T. S. might just qualify on that score. What I really want is for Tommy to come in contact with a first-rate mind, not just a dry-as-dust collector. Wisconsin, I well know, would provide just such an intellectual "atmosphere." Don't suppose Tommy would be up to your "Advanced Seminar: Meta-Biotics in Azulikulan," his first year, but might later. And if Tommy hit it off with Galpar, I don't doubt you could place him somewhere "out here."

Fact is, if Tommy could sign on with you-all at Galpar, then the tuition money in pocket would see the "Old Folks" to Europe. I'm ready to find out for once and for all about the relationship of Cave Ideographs to Impalic Migrations, from the Medieval point of view, of course. Thanks for the boost on that same project with the Ford Foundation; I understand we lost out in the final round. I'll try a Guggy, next year.

My best to your Squaw and your children. I guess your eldest boy is at Cal Tec? And liking it?

Just in passing, do you know anybody in the English Department at Penn State? I understand they really need a Chairman. Not that I'd exactly want to go there, but that happens to be Merle's home (Scranton). She's pressuring me to return to the womb. Also, to be honest, I find all of California d-u-l-l.

Shall we open a keg—of nails—sometime?
Cal

1020 Ketchell Terrace

Dear Puce:

Note change of address. It's a long story, but I'll tell you all about it over a drink, sometime.

Thanks for the help on the Tuition Scholarship at U of P . . . know you did your best. Tommy's plans are still a little up in the air, but he has several things lined up.

Looks like Castelvetro simply can't be made available to the Modern Mind: no Italy for Merle and myself. I've been thinking I'll just let it cool off, and later get a religious angle and try it on the Catholic-Center Foundation. Have times ever been so bad for Scholarship?

Best to the "gode wif" and Suzy and her fine twins. My, I'll bet she has her arms full!

I'm reading (for review) your "Caedmon: Hunter or Harpist." I'm giving it everything I've got, of course.

> Yr Obedient Ser,
> Farkesgill

1020 Ketchell Terrace

Dear Turnball:

Note change of address.

Sorry Tommy lost out in the finals on the Bob Jones, Jr., deals. Tom, very wisely it seems to me, decided to get through with his Service Obligation, and maybe get out before another Grass-Fire War breaks. Tommy wants the Armored Division, but Merle and myself think free training in languages or G-2 might be more fun. Tom always did have a flair for languages. I've written our Senator and tried to put the case lucidly.

No luck on my Merrie England project. "Arthur: King or Confidence Man" was turned down cold. If foundations can think so little of basic research, with the Russians and all, then perhaps I'll just have to shelve the whole thing, *sine qua non*.

Thought you might be amused to know about Puce's kid, Suzy. She brought her twins back home. The Gent in question, he gone! Where do we go from here, sez I. Scrutts's boy got the boot at Cal Tec, but got a Fellowship in his old man's field, Anthropology, *but* in Texas. J. D. wanted Harvard, I know.

Best to your "*Summum Bonum*." California still no good.

> *Vale!*
> Farkesgill

1020 Ketchell Terrace

Dear James Dudley:

I sincerely appreciate your effort on the "Grant-in-Aid" thing; really do. Knew you could swing it, if anyone could. Also, was happy to be of service in your son's case, and conclude it does no harm to be "well connected" at a place like Texas. Fine school. He'll like it.

You may know that our Tommy has had a "change of objective" as the educationalists put it.

To make a long story short, T. S. is finessing both college and graduate school, in favor of his Service Obligation. He has already done Basic (whatever they do there). He put in for the Armored Division but got the Quartermaster. You know any Generals in the Service branches?

Why he can't use the "Grant-in-Aid" is this: he met a grand girl, though a bit older than himself. They have a great deal in common, and that High Sierra scenery did it! Merle and myself are tickled to death, of course.

Note change of address: this girl Tommy married, just before he enlisted, had several brothers. The party, before the marriage—two nights before—got out of hand. We were not home, so never got the straight of it. Tommy didn't say, but I deduce something like this: the girl has four brothers, big fellows. They dropped by our house that night on some kind of business. One thing led to another, and they got to celebrating. The girl in question sided with her brothers—which is understandable—but T. S. is pretty handy with the old mitts. Soooo.

The cops got there about the same time we did. The neighbors were all watching, and someone turned the hose on everybody. But it was all in good fun. The wedding came off two days later, with all hands present or accounted for, and all smiles. Guess that's California for you, hey?

But you know how *sensitive* Merle is. Anyway I guess we didn't need a house, now that T. S. is in Service and living with his little new bride in what they call "Off Post." In short,

Merle said it was a very good time to leave the neighborhood. She found this apartment. And here we are.

Actually, I like it better in just two rooms: no yard work. My books, naturally, are in storage, so "Cave Ideographs and Impalic Migrations" will have to wait. In fact I told the Dean precisely *that*.

Actually, Jim, as the Dean told me, we value teaching a great deal "out here." You, yourself, have come around to this Wisdom: to Teach is to Live . . . something like that.

Of course I don't know about your field, but in mine the real bankruptcy of scholarship—*real* Scholarship—is too apparent in such items as, "Caedmon: Hunter or Harpist" and even Tuffy's latest, "Thomas Watson: Sage or Savage." What can one say, in print, to such tiny, forced things?

No matter, though, when the bell rings for next fall, you bet I'll be right in there eating chalk dust and "doing my damnest" to influence the Minds of This Generation. If not us, J. D., then who can do the job?

See you Christmas, at the convention!

Skoal!

Calvin Farkesgill

Ace in the Hole

Ace in the Hole

Everyone from the old outfit who could make it came to our Skipper's funeral.

We were together once more, and he was still in front of us with the American flag hanging fallow on its jack staff, and our spray of white and red carnations draped like a fresh, scented blanket across the upraised lid of his coffin. All the Quonset huts where so often he had briefed us for flight were gone now. Our final meeting place was in the square, dim room of a funeral parlor. An organ whistled softly.

In the old way, we were in ranks before him, trying not to rustle the gun-metal, open-mouthed chairs. Therefore the old discipline settled down upon us, even though our war was over, and even though all of us now alive had healed a long time ago.

Now we were old. Nothing more. Some of us went up in the world after our squadron disbanded, and those men had suits expensively cut to conceal a sly, gutty paunch. Some of us had slid down, and over the abyss, and into the Land of the Poor: those faces were hacked, and in those laps were the restless, red-puffed knuckles of poverty. Yet rich or poor, perhaps by some last minute strategy or theft, we wore white shirts.

In Corsica and in France even the mail orderly wore a red silk throat scarf. The Skipper had started that fad. Skip really was our leader.

For the last time the Skipper was in front of us and we were in the crude civilian ranks of lined-up chairs. We half expected him to shout At Ease, in the way he could do without offending what was left of our air crews.

Instead of our old Skipper rising to speak, a young Episcopal preacher appeared suddenly in the open space near the pulpit. The young man cleared his throat. The preacher did not seem quite ready for this job. That was appropriate. Even on this final mission, Skip would have to make out with an underage, green kid.

To make out: that was the entire history of Josie Squadron. And we did make out, or at least those of us who came back, and were now present or accounted for. Even Skip made out the best he could on that last day of his life. At least what he did that last day of his life was not done casually.

"Friends and members of the Squadron," the young priest said. He felt himself a stranger, and of course he was. Obviously he had checked out of Seminary for perhaps one year and been ordained not more than thirty days. "We are here to bury Harry . . ."

The unintentional rhyme of bury and Harry tripped the young man. Tripped up was the story of Josie Squadron, and it seemed that the young priest's remark could not have been otherwise.

From behind a light gauze curtain where Skip's old father and Skip's children were seated, I heard the faint, suppressed voice of a woman sobbing. That was Skip's wife, Josephine.

The night we named the squadron after her, we were drunk, of course. Skip did not object, though someone wanted to know if she, too, was a night fighter. From the

picture of Josie on Skip's desk, and from meeting her at
our squadron's "conventions" afterwards, I knew why "Josie
Squadron" was a lucky name. That night we activated the
squadron we were young and noisy, but privately each man
wondered how well that name would transmit on the R/T
when we might be lost at angels twelve, somewhere in those
nightmare clouds, calling Base, and trying not to sound afraid.

The young priest got bury, Harry, and carry into his second attempt. I turned to the man in ranks beside me: Cue
Mondale. We were tentmates at Albiers, during the worst
winter of all.

Cue winked. He was thinking the same thing: one more
time for Josie Squadron, situation normal . . .

I looked on down the row of men. Skip's old crew chief,
Lovett, now worked for a bus line, a master mechanic; beside him was Hacker, who married three wealthy women, one
after the other, and was now at Palm Beach where he had
always lived. An armorer, Yewell, had become a cop; he sat
next in ranks to Sneaky-Pete Flonnol, who was a bum in
Josie Squadron, and was now still a bum, out on parole.
Wierick and Scotal; Hedger and Lons: welders, executives,
wholesalers, TV repairmen, barkeepers, and at the far end of
the row was Speak-to-Me Bowles, in his own wheelchair, a
victim of arthritis. Mostly, however, we were what we had
always been, with a few here and there in the room broken
by circumstances they either did not know, or could not yet
recognize. Also there was me: from the day Skip came in to
take over Josie Squadron I was his Radar Op, and I never
rode behind a better pilot.

The preacher finally got his sermon airborne. From behind
the curtain of gauze the woman's voice stopped. In the way of
old soldiers who have heard it all before, each man thought
his own thoughts as we sat in rows in that pale-green room,
waiting for something to end.

Skip really was a leader. For him we did improbable
things. Yet he did more than anyone else, and got less
credit. He flew every other night, and then did all of the

administration. Without him, I suppose, the squadron would have dropped back into its hopeless bunks; no one would have bothered to get up in the mornings. It was ridiculous, but we flew our missions anyway. Afterwards, when the war was over, by way of the squadron "conventions," Harry could still hold us together. Now Harry was gone.

Oh, we were not a bad outfit. In fact we were almost marvels. But we were orphans, lost and buried and ignored in the vast administrative maelstrom of the war; we were detached, on special duty, administratively connected with a Base Section, and as our mess sergeant always said, attached only to God for rations.

We did what could be done, and we did it with airplanes even the British confessed were through. We seemed always the victim of some cruel administrative or tactical joke, but we flew out at night, and usually came back.

In England, where we sometimes went to steal spare parts, the hot pilots got off in Thunderbolts or in Spit IV's; those pilots wore flight jackets lined with red satin. In England the B-17 crews went out to a designated target, and came back, and painted a black cross on the nose of each airplane. Those gunners knocked the Focke-Wulfs and the 190's from the sky, and the German smoke and glycol streamed down like unfastened sacks of flour towards the pig-back earth. In England where we went to steal spare parts we saw the grand, public war. That war was not our war.

We lived in the mud. We flew off the mud and some steel matting near the town of Albiers. Of all things, we were an American nightfighter outfit. Although we were in the U. S. Air Force we flew British Bristol Beaufighters. For supplies we were attached to the French. Yes, the French. So we borrowed and swapped to get P-X rations, and even food. Every man in Josie Squadron was a good thief, and we signed the Skipper's name to anything. Once an old National Guard Colonel gave me a whole stack of .50 ammo. "Take hit all m'boy," he said grandly. "Them bastards of mine can't even open the boxes."

Every day some Air Force supply officer who treated airplanes as though they were shovels would say, "But *why* have you got Beaufighters? Why in the hell did they give you Beaus?"

The Beaufighters were good airplanes; snub nosed and deep chested, two radial engines in the wing roots, and behind the pilot a blister for the Radar Op. When we found an airborne target the radar man was supposed to steer the pilot into the target. When the pilot got a visual, he was supposed to ride on in. But Josie Squadron lacked the ground radar equipment, and the controllers who were supposed to vector us into the enemy planes. Therefore we flew night intruder missions, at low level, always down some nightmare valley, across the Rhine. The pilots seemed always to poke around in the rocks. We shot at anything that either moved, or was on fire.

At the end of a long day of stealing from some Infantry Division, and with the weather going sour, but still above limits, and with an airplane that was never exactly right, Skip would run up those thousand and forty-five horses locked in our wings. The engines were always good. Then Skip would call back through the interphone, "Red-Top, let's go to work?"

Then the radial engines pulled us up into the night, and probably into a rainstorm that might soon turn to ice.

One night in March we came back from Germany. We were low, as usual, looking for "opportunity." The Rhine was good for barges. You could see them against the water. That night a barge turned out to be a flak boat. Their gunners almost shot our starboard engine from its mounts. The weather was going sour, and we came low over Saarbrücken. The American flak opened up. Then on final approach, near Albiers, our own flak around our own field took a crack at us because our starboard engine was throwing sparks and yellow flame. The runway had a bad dip in the middle. We touched down fast, and the runway fell out from under our wheels.

At that moment, as the end of the runway came floating

towards my face, our tower's casual voice came in very
clearly:

Green Leader One is down.

Skip transmitted back, in the clear, "I'm not so god-damned
sure."

We hit hard once more, and bounced, and stopped—and
the gear collapsed.

But we made it. There were whole panels ripped off the airplane. Four days later we flew out once again into Germany,
at night.

During the entire war Josie Squadron did not shoot down
a single enemy plane. Skip always wanted one—just one. He
thought one enemy plane destroyed would justify his own
training. But we never did find it, though we always tried.
Toward the last there were not many German airplanes. We
damaged barges, and we burned trucks in convoy, and we
got one locomotive. Mostly we fought the terrifying weather
of northern France. Not a single one of the pilots had a
thousand hours in the air. Skip, himself, was the oldest man
in the whole outfit. Was he twenty-five years old, at the
time?

I suppose the memory of all those improbable things caused
us to smile a little when the young priest bogged down again,
just a little bit, toward the end. "So . . . we have come to bury
Harry, not to Harry carry . . ."

Skip would have laughed, but now he could hear nothing.
We were all sure of that. We put up with it until the priest
was almost finished. In a way, however, the young man was
gutty. He did not try to ignore the way things actually happened at the end.

". . . What Harry did, that final day of his life," the priest
said, "is thought in some religions to be a grievous sin. But,
gentlemen, if we can find it in our poor human hearts to
forgive this man who is here beside us, can not God forgive
Harry with infinitely greater compassion? We believe God
Almighty will do this. Therefore he will make right all
infirmity. . . ."

Once more I looked on down the row of men. We were all infirm, to be sure; I had always thought Skip was the strongest. But if some of the men were of a faith which did not condone what Skip had done, they did not let on.

Then the funeral was over.

I was glad.

We stood up, still in ranks. The green chairs rustled their little rubber feet on the carpet. A dozen men reached for cigarettes, but suddenly remembered not to smoke.

We filed past. During the sermon I had thought of Skip in uniform. Even his rank was a joke: he did the job of a light colonel, but only on his day of discharge was he anything more than a captain. We were nearly all captains. No promotions for Josie Squadron ever came through. But Skip was not now in uniform. He was in a medium-priced gray suit. They had rebuilt the side of his face.

No one changed expression as we filed past.

Then we were out of the pale-green room where the organ whistled softly. I knew we were also out of the old squadron forever. At last we were disbanded. Everyone knew it. Now we did not remember that we had helped win a war, and had lived, and had come back. Now we were the surplus generation, and there was nothing left of all that had happened except the mixed terror of our triumphs over weather, and over our own fear.

Outside the wind was colder than usual. March was trying to translate itself into one more April. Somewhere under the curbs and streets, under the anatomy of the sidewalk, I could still see the frozen mud of Albiers, at the time when April was always cruel.

"Hey Red-Top . . ."

I turned.

Henry Lever was also an old Radar Op. We had busted out of Cadets, and had gone on through Jockey school, to keep on the combat air crews.

Now we see each other once a year, at our "conventions." He lives somewhere out on Long Island, beyond Farmingdale.

"Drink?"

"Oh no," I said, and Henry was not disappointed. It was only eleven o'clock in the morning. The old men of Josie Squadron did not drink as much as they used to.

"Coffee?"

Although we had nothing much to hold us together, we still did not want to part. We knew this was the breakup of our final camp.

"No doughnuts," I said.

Henry nodded. We were both keeping an eye on our weight. Quietly, we sat there in the booth. Henry was in a broker's office. I was a credit manager for the telephone company. We had both taken a little time off for Skip's funeral. We would both go back to work after lunch.

For the last time, we talked about Skip.

"He *was* a hard-luck man," Henry said. But he added, "You would know. You flew with him."

I heard the wind whistling through our lowered gear and flaps. I heard a Beaufighter, on final approach; I saw all that flak, and our own boundary lights, and the flares winking past the corners of my eyes, growing brighter. *Green Leader One is down* . . .

"Not hard luck," I said. "Skip just made out with what we had. He made out better than anyone else could have."

"I guess he liked it."

"Yes," I said, but I was not certain about that, any more. To be loyal I said, "Yes, he sure did."

"Why didn't he stay in?"

Henry did not know of the time after the war was over, late at night, when I went into Skip's tent. At the time the squadron was waiting to be moved some place, just any place.

Skip had applied for the regular Air Force, but they turned him down. Already his eyes were beginning to go. He never could have made out with jets. As airplanes were made to fall in great flapping chunks of metal from the sky, or were made to burn brightly through the fog that concealed some final hillside, so were some pilots trained to be used in that way. Even before the war was over, Skip's kind was already finished. Skip was too old, almost twenty-seven.

"Physical," I said.

"Oh."

Skip, too, had known he was finished. He always saw things clearly. He tossed the paper to me as I stood in the door of his tent, and he said,

"Red-Top, I've had it on aircraft."

Finally we all came back to the States. Josie Squadron also had it. The old outfit was only a piece of paper in a file, somewhere in a file box beside other file boxes, perhaps in some government warehouse, perhaps in St. Louis.

Naturally, Skip was elected president of Josie Squadron Organization; he ran the "conventions." He started well in civilian life: became an architect. Skip had his own firm, in a little town in New Jersey.

"I can forgive him," I told Henry, "and I am sure God will—as the young man back at the funeral parlor said."

Henry knew and I knew and Skip knew that God had nothing at all to do with this. Henry knew and I knew that when Skip walked out into the rock garden behind his house that afternoon, he had hesitated not at all. We had been trained to attack, and the habits were with us because in bad weather a man grows old and what is learned in youth is confirmed by the ritual fires of the antiaircraft shells going off somewhere below the leading edge of the wing, all in a row, like fiery dancers.

"But could you do what Skip did?"

Henry looked at me across the top of a very safe table, as though I were a savage. In a way we were all savages, and that was as it should be, for in our forced growth somewhere between the mud and the ice-forming weather we had lost what we never had, a fear of opinion, and the easy reliance on authority.

"No—no," I said. I was remembering my own wife and three daughters at home, all red-headed. "No, I couldn't do what Skip did. It's just not in me, Henry."

"Even if you had what Skip had? Even if you knew you had bought the farm, at last, and it was a matter of three more bad months? Even if you *knew* what you had was really terminal?"

I thought again of my own wife, and the children. I wavered, and then I knew.

"Couldn't do it," I told Henry. "I was never quick enough on the big decisions. That's why I rode behind. I could never do it. Especially at noon. In clear weather."

Henry looked at me strangely, and did not say anything.

... The weather: no one in Josie Squadron will ever forget the weather. The mildest day of summer I still look up and see those terrifying clouds and I still think of some airman lost, calling Base, and the static coming in, like rocks in your ears. It's different now, of course.

Then Henry got up, and I got up.

Though Henry had found me out, we looked together at the clock on the wall of the restaurant. Already too much time, like some precious, liquid metal, had pumped through that unyielding dial.

We shook hands. Good-by.

Without hesitation, Henry walked out of the small restaurant, and into the street.

I hesitated at the cash register. Then I paid my bill. I paid this bill as we seem to pay all our bills. Only a little change was given back to me in the green, shiny, plastic dish. But I took every coin. I clawed at the bottom of the dish, and I grasped for it all.

I stood for a second in the door, staring ahead through the glass. I hesitated, and outside I saw many people walking, each man with his head bent forward, staring into the sidewalk.

I took a deep breath, as though I were at the edge of some strange, cold, glaucous pool where the water was deep and roiled by the unseen violence of underwater swimmers, somewhere ahead, somewhere I could not see.

I too opened the door.

I stepped out into that brief, flightless, unyielding street of middle age.

The Freezer Bandit

The Freezer Bandit

See the boy's picture on page one but not me. Why?

Why not see this building from the outside where arrow points to window, or interior where he calmly awaits or see about my important work which people do not realize. Important but people do not *realize* the whole *Truth*. Why?

Why, because you don't know but every week in the papers you have been reading about my work. And I'll tell you the real Truth: ever see those advertisements for a Freezer Plan?

I know all about the terms and the deal because I telephone the salesmen and ask them to come to my room, right here on Front Street, beside the river. When the salesman come up the stairs I say I have been reading their ads.

"Good, good," they all say, and they unbuckle the brief-case and begin to scatter literature on the floor of my room.

"Save you thirty two percent on your food bills," they say, but I get them started on the freezer itself, about the lights inside. And about the door lock.

You would be surprised how many women sell freezers

and *not one* ever asks about my family or *what am I going to feed*. I live alone and yet I want the side of beef, but they are so intent on their own profit they never think to help others. Why? Even if I do live alone and have no family at all you can't accuse me of being selfish.

And then I say, "Could you name a satisfied customer?"

You would be surprised how many names they give me for my list.

After these salesmen leave I sit in the dark and stare at the four-color literature scattered on the floor. Barefooted, I walk on the pictures of all those different freezers. In the darkness you can imagine that pictures are the real thing.

Also my outside work.

The freezer-plan people have two plants here in the city. Very early on nice days I go to their Eastside plant. A food-plan delivery truck will stop about twenty minutes to service a home freezer. Once I pick up the driver's route I can walk along behind and note down the house numbers. I never loiter but I see things, and you would be surprised how many people—men and women—keep a freezer *in the basement*. Naturally that means a nice driveway, and a side door. If a dog I mark "D" on my list.

Sometimes during the week I transfer all my numbers to a map of the city, which I keep on the wall of my room. That gives me a *plan* of my own. When I get a nice pattern of numbers say out in Dolphwood, or Linden Acres, I begin to walk at night.

You would be surprised what you see through their windows. Maybe the other ones I pass also walking at night would do it, but I never leave the sidewalks unless I intend to see their freezer. It's a rule. Also I never loiter. Just the same, you can see plenty.

The other night I saw a dog run across a picture window. Right behind the dog I saw this woman, with a robe on, chasing the dog. Now did she want the dog, or had it done something on the floor, or had she caught it sniffing around her freezer, or what?

My patterns on my map tell me which streets to walk. I carry a self-addressed package because in case I am stopped for identification purposes only I am out mailing something, see? I have never been stopped or molested in any way in those new areas where all the freezers are, but just the same I carry a package all wrapped and stamped even at two o'clock in the morning. Probably you have seen me walking out there sometime but just didn't know who it was.

Well, pretty soon I know by sight all of the houses on my list in, say, Linden Acres.

This next step in my important work may seem a little unusual. In fact I myself know better ways to determine which place I want to enter, to see their freezer. For example, I could telephone to find if anyone is home, *et cetera, et cetera*. But here is the way I actually work. After walking at night for a couple of weeks, I begin to *know* which places are ready for me. Perhaps it is the shape of the roof or a gable thrust up toward the sky or perhaps it's the curved vaginal shape of the driveway that tells me. But when I walk past a house for perhaps the tenth time, I know. At this moment I get a feeling of satisfaction, as though I have already seen their freezer. After I get that feeling, nothing can keep me out.

Not that I'm a nut, or anything like that! But normally speaking, I'll see their freezer. After all I'm only human, so you can't expect the impossible.

When I *know* a place is ready for me I go back across town to my room to get my tools.

When you are in your room beside the river with the shade pulled down and when you open your closet and lay your suit on the bed and when you remove the secret plywood panel in the back of the closet you can bring out your tools; it is the beginning. Many a time I have pulled on my pigskin work gloves and have stood in the center of this room with the automobile jack in my hand. Just standing there for a moment gives you a funny feeling, something very much like the satisfaction of knowing a basement is ready for you.

All my tools fit into the suitcases. I constructed the suitcases especially to fit the tools (regards length, balance, et
cetera). Those two suitcases appear very heavy, and I've
caught people staring when I carry them through a crowd.
Actually those people who stare are wrong. My two foil-
lined cases are very light, and the little straps on the inside
keep my pinch bars and speed drill in place.

With a suitcase in each hand I walk back across town.
When I get closer to the places I have in mind, I keep to the
side streets and I make myself take very short steps.

Very slowly, I walk past once, to let the house decide. If
the car is gone, that's a good sign. But if ever I start up the
drive I go quickly and directly to the basement door. And
I'll tell you one thing: a lot of people out in Trotwood leave
their basement doors unlocked. This makes me sore. Everyone ought to lock up, especially if they have kids or a freezer.

For a moment beside the locked door in the darkness, it is
nice. But I get out the pinch or the key ring or the glass
cutter and my putty knife. If the door says no one is home
at all I don't mind a little noise. Did you ever put a bumper
jack against a really solid door and then work the handle
back and forth until there is a shiver, and the splinter, inside,
of a door jamb?

The moment I push the suitcase through a splintered door
and walk into a basement, I can always see a freezer of any
kind—chest, upright, or what have you.

Regards freezers. All freezers have locks, let's say. The lock
is usually right in the handle and the manufacturer and the
manufacturer's engineers actually put the lock in the handle
to be locked. I've read all the factory manuals and I've borrowed lots of booklets out of the freezers on the floors
of appliance shops and in every case the manufacturer
intended the lock *to be used*. Those locks make a lot of sense.
They keep out Unauthorized Personnel. When I, myself, have
a real freezer I will certainly keep it locked At All Times.

Well, you feel all over the box. You see the kind of wall
which is behind, and the kind of floor underneath. On a chest

type you simply put the automobile jack on the floor, and then work the handle of the jack back and forth. The freezer is heavy, and you can feel the lid begin to quiver. Then everything lets go.

With an upright, it is different. You feel all over the box and you secure the box with the little windlass and the stainless steel cables and you use the wedge and keepers so the jack can get some purchase on the door. Then you work the jack handle back and forth and back and forth and the big flat door begins to quiver. *Whoomb*, everything lets go.

The light inside the freezer comes on, and the cold rush of air flows out and around your feet as though you were standing suddenly in cold water that you can not actually see near the ocean. The motor begins to race, as though it is frightened. You have done it again.

You see everything: the frosty shelves, the aluminum grills, and baskets, and coils that curl around the frozen packages and shimmer in the light. For a second I stand in the shadows, then I put away my tools. I keep one eye on the frozen world, the gorge, the cold antiseptic landscape of an opened freezer in its own approving light. *Yes.*

You see three kinds of freezers. First, they may be full of homemade stuff, cookie dough, and it is not neat or orderly. They could get in on a Food Plan but they don't. Why?

The second kind of freezer is the way the brochures show it: orange juice, grapefruit juice, grape juice, pineapple juice, orange-grapefruit-pineapple juice, mixed in one can, all in even rows. Then the broccoli and asparagus and French-cut or Regular beans, and Brussel sprouts, and black-eyed peas and Regular peas and carrots and Peas mixed. Then the frozen grits, and TV dinners, and Italian Plates, and Mexican Plates, the Shore Platter, and the UN Special, which is everything on one tin foil plate. Finally, on the bottom, the meats: head cheese, and bologna; steaks and chops; lights and tripe and kidneys; ox tails, soup bones, hamburger, pork links, veal patties, mock chicken, and city chicken, and fryers and two Sage hens, and maybe a pheasant in a cellophane bag. It's the Full Freezer, the American dream where there is no work and 32 per cent off on your food bills and that's the big idea, if you see what I mean.

But the third kind. Someone ought to put a stop to it. The freezer you open is locked, but empty. I mean it. Empty. They have the freezer and they could get in on a Food Plan and that is why I'm telling you this, because there are so many empty freezers. Why?

In Brentwood, and Trotwood, and Arkham Heights I find all freezers belong to a Freezer Plan but when the door quivers and those nice white lights come on like the inside of a hospital where they wheel you down the curved cor- ridors and into the tile-lined coil-lighted operating room or to where the ice bath is you find—after all—the freezer is empty. When I find an empty freezer I think something is wrong with the whole system: the two packing plants, the dogs that like to follow the delivery men right into the kitchen, and the Plan itself. Some day all freezers *will stop working*.

People ought to realize this.

But when a freezer is what it ought to be, I take my broc- coli and soup bones and juice. The moment I walk out of a basement I have a nice little food plan, in miniature, packed in my foil-lined cases. I walk across the city to my room, and unload, and then walk back again to get the items I left hid- den under the shrubbery. Two trips will clean out any freezer. Then I get some sleep.

You think I would eat that stuff?

Not on your life. And I can explain that, too.

Before anything melts, I take a *very few* packages to vari- ous outlets. I get my coffee and bread and hot dogs in ex- change. Naturally I get a little cash, extra.

I'm saving all the cash to get a nice upright of my own because if you think I like to get names on a list, and walk at night, and keep a map, and carry two suitcases across the city, you are crazy. Like everyone else, I want to take it easy.

When I save enough cash I'll set an upright in my room and every night I'll take a look . . . After all, I'm only human.

Regards the other packages of frozen things, which I mentioned.

This next may strike you a little odd, until you think about it. You may have wondered about all those shelves, from top to bottom, in the closet where I keep my tools. Those shelves are built just right to hold juice, and vegetables, and TV dinners, and all my meats. That closet is my Ever Normal Granary. A light comes on when you open the door and I put foil on the walls and rubber sheeting on the floor. Naturally, however, my stuff melts, thaws out, turns to water. It's not fair or right: some of us have got no juice. *We are cut off from the cold.* Why? Some of us don't have either the Plan or the freezer. Why?

I want you to know this: though I have to keep bringing in more things (because I have not yet saved enough) I do not waste food. As the packages on the bottom of my closet melt, I place them by my window. I sit there at night and one by one I throw every single item back into the river. *Back* to the river. Water makes vegetables, and the river is water, so I give everything back to the river. I am probably the only individual you know that feeds rivers.

Now, about that boy.

First, off, I want you to know I did not *encourage* him. He really wanted to do it, and I'll tell you all about that.

I was in the Arkham Heights district. I had my suitcases and all my tools. There was a nice curved drive toward the basement door, and lots of soft bushes.

Upstairs in this house was a party. I like to watch a party as well as the next individual. I saw a woman run past the window, and a man run right after her. There were about thirty couples, dancing and touching each other in various ways.

Outside the basement door I listened. The place wanted me too.

But not locked.

A forty-thousand-dollar house and a big freezer in the basement and they don't lock the basement door. That one made me sore: everybody should lock their basement doors.

Sure enough, in the corner a big white upright freezer was breathing ever so lightly. I could already feel the quiver that comes when my automobile jack gets good purchase on a door. Directly above my head was the music and the dancing, not three feet away. If they had only known what was just below their feet . . .

Freezer not locked. That one really made me sore. Of course I take a look at freezers because that's where all the stuff is. But if a freezer is not locked then I might as well *do it* in an appliance store . . .

Cold air gushed out. The inside service light flickered on.

There she was: corridors of tile and frost and the hospital smell of an electric motor. The sterile cold air was the ether and the cold of the Veterans' Hospital ice bath where they used to soak me.

Empty. Not a package of broccoli or asparagus or juice or even a lousy homemade cake or those phoney roasting ears that a lot of individuals put up in plastic bags. For a moment I just stood there, very angry thinking I was alone, you see what I mean?

"You stealing stuff?" this kid says, from behind me.

I was a little surprised.

I turned around.

You saw him on page one, but now he was astraddle my large suitcase, like on a hobby horse. Right away I knew he had followed me through the basement door, else wouldn't I have heard him when he walked down the stairs to see the freezer before he went to bed?

"Oh yeah?" the kid says and rocked back and forth on my large suitcase and said giddy-yap as on TV but then he got off and came and stood beside me—like this—and looked inside the freezer. Black hair and black eyes, and about this tall, about up to the second shelf. Either he was smoking a cigarette or his breath was turning white in the cold air that came out of the freezer. No kid should smoke. I mean cancer is just everywhere.

"Sure," I said very kindly because I saw he was interested in the same thing I was. "My tools are in the suitcase. Service call."

"I'll bet," the kid says, and booted my black suitcase. "At two A.M.?"

In all the years I have been walking at night and getting lists of names by following along behind the freezer delivery-men, doing this very important work, no one ever saw me. Oh, barked at by dogs and I've slipped back into corners to hide when women unexpectedly came down the basement steps, but this kid is the first individual who ever came on me when a freezer door was open and lighted.

"Three nights I been trailing you," the boy said and he came back to stand beside me. He was real interested, I could see that. "You nutty or something?"

"No I'm not nutty or something," I said.

The boy placed his hand on the cold shelf of the freezer. I saw that calm look on his face. He also liked to see a freezer. Perhaps in a slightly different way from me, a grown man, but he liked it. Right then I knew I wanted to tell him all about it.

You can recognize people who are like that boy. Sometimes around the bus station or the railroad station where I check my big suitcase I like to look directly into the faces of certain individuals. I think to myself, Oh the things I could tell you. If you just *knew* if you just knew how it is to let a frozen package of broccoli curve out the window and into that warm, soft river. Sometimes I look into a woman's face—especially—and I know she too would like to take a look at a freezer, but I don't ever ask any of them. I just think to myself: Oh, the things I could tell you if you just *knew* who I am.

"Empty," the boy says. "They signed up but they couldn't pay. Owe everybody in town."

I could see the kid was sore, too. I'm only human but that's too much: get a nice freezer and subscribe to the Plan, and then have an empty. Right then I knew if he was interested enough to follow me at night that I should teach him something that would do him some good in afterlife.

So I explained why every freezer should have something in it. Insofar as individuals do not follow the Plan then there is waste and inefficiency and a rise in temperatures and a general softening of the whole moral fiber of the U. S.

"And that is why," I told him just as plain as I'm telling you right now, "No one should ever *get inside*. In fact no individual has ever got inside a freezer."

"That so?" he says, and puts his hand back on the shelf, just to test the frost.

"Oftentime," I said, for I wanted him to understand about my work, "I myself, have thought it would teach everyone a good lesson."

He understood that all right. I wanted to teach him *one thing* and he understood. But I was ready to go now, and was just about to slam the door.

"Well," he said and he grabbed me by the arm and pulled me back, "I'm not as big as you and maybe I could . . ."

I did not encourage him. I said just what I'd tell any individual, namely, that no one should *ever get inside*. No matter what it would teach a lot of people.

"I'd do it," he said, "but does that little light go off?"

I was honest with him because I knew he had an interest. Frankly I do not know what happens inside so that's what I said.

"I do not know," I said, "Freezers are a hobby of mine you might say, but I would not know about the little service light."

Now that's exactly what I started to tell you, I mean the whole *Truth*: I did not encourage him.

His face was calm and smiling the last time I saw it. The latch made a very soft little click as I closed the door.

But here is the funny thing.

I never did find out from him if the light went off or not.

Just then the cars outside the house began to start. I had to get back across town to my room with the two black, empty suitcases.

Well, upstairs the people finally got over their party and got around to ordering, and a Food Plan delivery truck individual went into the basement. And opened the door. Which *was not locked*.

You have been reading in the papers how the boy shut himself in, which is correct. Also the people having the party upstairs did not come down to look inside their freezer before they went to bed, and they should always do that. It makes a real difference.

And that is why I have not been outside my room for three weeks. I have had to eat the frozen stuff I got from a little nine-footer out in Dolphwood. The old basis of exchange is gone because the clerks at those certain outlets now look at me in a very strange way. Why?

Therefore my river outside gets nothing but empty pasteboard boxes. Even now I hear the rains coming once more and the river is rising slowly. I cannot sleep because whenever I doze the river comes in my window to get at my foil-lined suitcases. Why?

But one of these nights I will have to go out. I still have a few names on the old list. In fact, I may get out your way.

Be sure to tell this to your daughters and to your wife: tell them, *keep their basements locked*.

You see what I mean?

The Antennae, and
the Race

The Antennae, and
the Race

Outside the hardware store, this side of the street from where
the jeweler pried off the back of the watch and pointed his
eye into the case while the movement ticked on a few minutes, Merle paused; in front of his newest display, where he
had worked since 10 A.M. in the dry window, he stopped. In a
second he would turn—as he always would until he died of a
heart attack—turn again to their house, and the "lunch" and
what was now in their basement.

Around him this town: in front of the bank two children
manipulated the water fountain and clear innocent water
arched up and into their mouths, or fell with a shattering
noise upon the street. Like an apparition a stripped-down
car slued into this street. It bounced near the curb where
two hired hands were loafing. They did not observe the
driver as he leaped out quickly as though the engine might
explode.

—Now would she make it to Cincinnati? Unk said.

—Yes, and Hoskins speculated upon this wheel neither of
them had seen before.—She would. Mayhap to Greensburg.

And here the discussion ended.

These things happened simultaneously among the uneven heat waves of the pavement as he faced the window display of their hardware store. But he only thought, Fall, again.

His men of clay were behind glass in their excelsior duck blinds, pointing their guns at the giant decoys afloat upon the lake of mirrors. Behind his artificial cattails he had stacked hundreds of shotgun shells, the limp, redlined jackets, and finally against the rear wall the merchandise his brother Harry insisted be on display: a solid bank of Winchester pump guns, black, ruthless.

This latest window would stop the farmers and the town's inveterate hunters this Saturday night. He called this creation "The Big Ones." He did not think, however, there was something both grotesque and comic about the small men in the blinds, aiming gallantly at the overwhelming decoys, unmoved and stately upon their round mirror lake. Or was this window Apparition Land where the foothills were piles of shotgun shells, and the forests were black Winchesters all in a row . . .

Since they had brought him home again he'd done nothing but sleep and work a little in this largest window of the family store. Harry encouraged this sometimes. He arranged Summer with camping equipment, and did Spring with piles of seed. This square pane of glass was unchanging. He was free to choose, limited only by the contents of the store itself. Nor did he consider the possibility of going any farther for materials than their warehouse in the rear of the building, to the sheds from which the owl-front store had grown. Therefore he both chose and received his materials from the store shelves, and the parts' bins, and gave no thought of sources, or limitations, or to the possibility that he, himself, was also of the shelves, or of the warehouses where bats flitted among black soil pipe. He thought now upon this window and on the Christmas season when he would use deep swirling battens of snow and black light and a chromium toaster suspended, turning steadily, like a planet.

He turned away then, and walked through the noon of

October toward the residential part of town which lay in a grove of oaks across the railroad. He walked stiffly, as though his loins were in a corset. He needed to watch the heart now, they had said. As he walked he removed his terse Panama hat, and wiped sweat from the wen that seemed to ooze from under the folds of skin above his red, left, drooping eyelid. A neon Beer sign wriggled like a red serpent at the level of his eyes. In the drugstore trash piled on the sidewalk the unmistakable snout of an empty whisky bottle thrust up from among boxes. He looked at it, only, and with a skittish nod of the head walked almost briskly past.

Oh Harry and Harry's packing-box wife, Eloise, had taken him during the Christmas rush to the place near Chicago. The Indiana landscape and Rushville floated past their car windows. He saw a roadhouse sign wink, Cocktails. By afternoon, though, he had walked into the "Doctor's" office and Harry and Eloise said, "We've got to get back to Seville to take—ah—inventory."

They bowed and said nearly together, we've done everything we can. He disliked Eloise, but she "understood him so well," that his dislike was always secret, and therefore nearly Christian. Write, or call (yes, call). We will come and get you (yes, we will get you). They disappeared, floated in a car just above the driveway toward the iron gates where the watchman dozed.

He felt a little rocky, alone in the waiting room. These last six months before Christmas revolved steadily in his vision, like the winking spokes of a wheel. Every half hour during the whole summer he had been "just stepping out a second" to the Oasis Cafe. During the last shopping week before Christmas, when the extra clerks were frowzy and tired and smiling inwardly about their pay checks, there was only sixty-cents in his own cash drawer. Some others were short, too, for he didn't always take it from his own.

Well, hell, Harry, had said again, what would the Old Man say? Y'know *he* built up this whole outfit from practically a horse collar and a keg of nails. You have got to . . . y'know?

Certainly would straighten up, Harry, certainly would.

Then he began to give things away. Lucas you need a hay-fork; hell, take it. Strider you want a bicycle; take it. Foster needs a stove; why, go ahead, it's the Season, isn't it? Some people said, I'll pay Harry anyway. They snapped open a black purse and shoats came squealing out.

The night before Christmas his wife had gone back to Cincinnati. He did not blame her. They had met in a bar, and when they were married he found she could not be alone ever, and he couldn't be in two or three places at the same time. She went back to Mariemont to her father. She sat all day in the window by herself, looking out, for she had mastered, finally, how to drink alone. All of this had con-sumed fifteen years, and Hell's own new automobiles smashed. They always drank when they drove.

Even before high school, there had been the Founder, the old man. He was short and cherubic. He had been a grocery clerk and had sold hardware on the road and had opened an earlier version of this same store when he was only twenty-two. He always pranced between the counters, or went as though on ice. The iron shelves and scythes, the mop handles and the sharp edges of butt hinges never slowed him down. Even after all those years he still came in, especially at Christ-mas. Harry said to the customers, Oh yes, Pop is very active for his age. Gets stronger every day.

Merle, the elder brother, had always known, he was to "carry on." But Harry was the one who could sell iceboxes to the Eskimos, the customers always said. He sold radios when they came in, and bottled-gas stoves, when they came in; now at fifty years of age he was all for television. College, Merle knew, had never been out of the question for the Founder had offered to send him to Business School in Columbus. Yes, had offered to send him to Business School in Columbus. Yes, had offered, pleaded in fact. By then he liked only to sleep on the roof in the sunshine, dozing high above the town, squinting along his finger at the silver water tower in the afternoon, peering over the roof edge at a drummer alighting in front of the Hotel, carrying a white sample case. When high school was over he sensed he was not taken seriously any more and that was what he wanted but could not accept even when he was twenty-two.

In the end Harry and Eloise had to take a complete inventory. They tried to see what he had given away; would find out what had been sold at night in an alley behind the store or perhaps traded in the alley for rotgut.

He was alone in the waiting room, musing on these things, feeling as though he were in a hospital amphitheatre under arctic lights waiting for the arrival of surgeons.

The nurse opened an abrupt door. Glittering in her hand and throwing wealth and ransom in sparkles—on the walls and ceiling and underfoot—he saw a bottle.

The Nurse placed the Rye precisely upon the white table in front of him.

He had thought there would be No Liquor Allowed On These Premises. Yet the quart bottle—(not a fifth)—was before him. The nurse worked leisurely at the government seals around the neck. Then the cork.

—A long, hot trip? she said and nodded her own answer, yes. She opened the panel cabinet on the wall and from among the stacked towels and adhesive tape rolls, she plucked out— a shot glass.

She seized the bottle. The liquor filled the glass up, up, as though she would run it over. The odor reached and found and touched him on the face. It was as though he had plunged to his shoulders into some unseen thicket of wild thyme. Through this spreading bouquet was the passage and the window to other worlds: you held the breath, and walked completely through Springtime until the foot did sweetly slide, and the forest gave easily the moss and roots of sleep. . . .

What land it was, or if these were only distant shores thereof, or if he remembered at all, he did not know; perhaps it was always suspended vaguely near the eye, unseen, yet beckoning like hunger.

—Yes, a long hard trip, Mr. Cohler. Will you have a drink?
He knew this had sustained him. He knew he had depended

for months, upon this, like a child upon its mother. He had at
first schemed, then lied, and finally had stolen for this; this
sweet violent smell of mint, or of a woman's belly. So he
said,

—Yes, I believe I will.

—And another?

—Yes. I just believe I will.

He did walk, it seemed, and was immersed to his shoulders,
and then he was through the thicket of wild thyme where the
vision was: the architects in eye shades drawing and dreaming
at tables; their builders at work upon the lowland of storage
sheds; the completed landscape of smokestacks, the environs
of cities, all distilling, distilling, distilling. Here at the end of
all, all industrial cunning he saw the product: here shimmering in the white drifts, spinning like some sweet unfolding
flower, the liquor.

He drank again, and felt better.

Later the nurse was saying,

—And another? We have plenty here at Maplegrove.

—There is?

—Now sir, once more.

She was larger, towering over him. He had noticed in the
past two hours how beefy the arms were. She was squat,
clucking. She bent over his thin, meatless neck. She put her
hands and her breath upon his delicate, protruding shoulder
blades. She liked to handle them rough, at first.

—No. No more formethanks.

—But you will. You must, and you shall! She bullied him,
triumphant.

Soon there was only one light far away, buzzing at him. He
knew he was going. . . .

Then he saw their bowl. For the first time. It was scarlet
on the outside, level with his eye. Inside there were white
concentric industrial gradations, up the side to the overflow
lip.

She struck him viciously in the belly. The whisky rose in
his throat like heavy, industrial, oils.

—Now: you must fill to our first day's mark. Later you will do better. Now here, you! Drink one more.

He cursed. But he drank.

Early the next morning the first nurse came and pulled him out of bed. It was the same thing all over again.

When Harry and Eloise came to fetch him three months later, he noticed how closely they watched him. He did not think they noticed he had lost much weight, or that the skin on his face was tired, as though the skin no longer cared whether or not it clung to the cheekbones.

On the way back to Ohio they stopped at a roadhouse. A waitress carried a tray of Old Fashioneds past their booth.

He smiled as he caught them staring at his lips. It's all right he said, I don't really want any. His eyelid drooped, and he raised his whole head as though he were encouraging the eyeball to look. He was not at all surprised that he did not want any: he really desired nothing at all. Once he had felt whisky was the most refined, the subtlest of all hardware, some liquid version of a new expensive, chromed blender sparkling in sunlight. Well, it was better this way. Perhaps now he would do one worthwhile thing. . . .

Back home, on the streets, or in the hardware store, in front of the bank, some were glad to see him looking better. As she passed Mrs. Biggs said be strong, be *strong!* The Moonshiner and his two slouching boys came in to buy a T-square, and to their question he said, I'm feeling some better. The Moonshiner, in his old felt hat, saw how it was; he did not mention the new run. He said, well, we-ahr might glad to hear of it. Harry also had seen the Moonshiner come in. At closing time Harry asked in his jolly manner, Well, how is it going, Old Settler? And Merle had replied, Oh all right.

By now, though, he had turned from the decorated store window and had walked through the town; he was across the railroad tracks, turning down Greentree Street. Once more he was facing the old folks' house, and the "lunch" she would almost have on the table. Their house (he had lived with them since coming back from Maplegrove Home, near Chicago) was a monastery of gables, aggressively well painted. In an upstairs window, beneath a cupola, was the Founder. He was in his straight-backed chair, his round shining face half visible from behind a hardware catalogue. He was considering Christmas merchandise. Though he creaked his chair, and cleared his throat, and bullied his mind, he could not decide upon the damned appliances.

Mother opened the door. She was put together with springs and burlap skin. She leaped from one part of her kitchen to the other: from her new washer and drier to the electric stove; from the juicer, the grater, the slicer, to her knife-sharpener.

"Oh, son, did you have a good morning?" She kissed him and smelled his breath at the same time.

"It's all right, Mother," he said fretfully.

He saw for the first time that her face was very much like that of a smiling spaniel. She was a dog lover, but she never thought to feed the dog in the basement.

"Your lunch is all ready," she said, and again he concluded from her tone that it was, as always, a heavy task. She pointed to the newest toaster and to the pile of loose bread. He wanted a glass of water, but decided to wait until she left the room—if she would only leave him by himself for a second.

Each time she looked at him, she denied her own suspicions. Always she got her nose, by an affectionate gesture, near his lips. When she knew there was no whisky odor for one more day, she would suddenly become active: straightening rugs with her toe, getting out the stale bread she used for toast at noon. She wagged and growled around the kitchen and he realized she would live to be one hundred years old. At least another twenty years. He was certain, and even this did not seem to matter.

Precisely, that odor came to him once more. From the upstairs dormers, down through the bathroom, and especially from their bedroom where he knew they still slept together and talked together late into the night about appliances or Harry and Eloise he smelled it. It was the smell of old people, or some grandmother's house at the edge of a village, the

odor of all the sickrooms he had ever entered, of his grand-
father's bearded funeral, when they lifted him up to look in
the coffin.

"*I* certainly don't smell anything," she said. "You're always
smelling something. My nose is much better than even your
father's."

He could see it in her face, behind the spring-clipped
jaws: if you don't like my house . . . and if you smell something, simply *try* to move out, just try. She understood perfectly: she had insisted he move in with them, into her house.
She knew that he could not be interested in moving else-
where.

She tried not to rattle the ice cubes in her own glass. She
wished she were having something besides her orangeade—
perhaps a broth. He did eat so little, but then he had been
very sick, no doubt. Oh it had cost them all a penny to send
him off to that rest home.

"There *is* something," he said with conviction after he
nibbled two pieces of toast and ruined a pancake she had
made from yesterday's batter. "I smell it."

He got up and left her in her kitchen.

He went down the basement steps, where their dog stayed.
In the darkness, among the rakes and hoes and extra lawn
mowers all oiled and wrapped against rust, he found it. Of
course he knew he would find it.

Four nights ago he had tossed and twisted on his bed. He
slept on the couch made up for him in the front room. She
always made it up as a sign they were retiring. She made it up
slowly and folded in her sighs . . . Oh, I'm getting old. . . .

He had heard their bed rattling in their own room directly
above him. They were twisting, rolling in the hot coils of
their sheets. Oh they were senile now, but sometimes their
bed rattled and plunged in the windy torment of their con-
versation. . . .

He had gotten up from his couch, where he could only lie
awake half the night, thinking of nothing at all. He had gone
up their stairs and had listened outside their door. He had
resisted the suggestion that came to him: enter, now. Inside,

as if they were dead, he heard nothing, nothing at all. Then he went downstairs to their basement.

In the dark basement, deftly, with the hands of a craftsman, he gripped the neck, just behind the toothless jaws. Artistically, rhythmically, he clenched his long fingers. His arms were strong, strong, at the moment. He did not weaken when he felt the shocking, mangy hair—like clay to be shaped—between his fingers. He raised it to the ceiling. In the unyielding dark square of their basement which framed them, he slammed it against the cellar wall. He covered the body with wrapping paper.

He was neither ashamed nor remorseful. His heart thumped as though the valves might tear suddenly and flood his own chest with the wild pumping. The stairs revolved. He speculated upon the future, some inexorable, blinking wheel. He read this blinking wheel and thought rationally: no, he would not kill them. He really wouldn't. Here the discussion ended.

And yet he wanted, deep within him, adulation. Only a very little. Their blind old dog that he, alone, would feed each day did not matter. It really didn't. At least the old dog had not starved.

"Old Age, I guess, Mother" was all he said when he came back up the basement stairs to finish his lunch. He carried his little present to her. In his arms.

He dumped the swelling, indecent body on her drainboard.

He turned from her open mouth that steel springs had not yet closed. He turned from her and the swollen body and the Founder and from their buzzing, clicking house. He opened another door: inside their lighted refrigerator was the ginger ale and all the orangeade bottles and the trussed carcass of the chicken for Sunday.

He deliberately poured one half glass of ice water. He paused and faced the cold, frosted, death-world inside their refrigerator door.

He wondered how everyone would like the big window, where the ducks were.

A View of the Beach

A View of the Beach

Into Kentucky, between Burley leaf and the blue grass she steered us, and Kentucky gave us wonders through her lecturing tongue. She was a schoolteacher on vacation and now the things she always had written on blackboards were just beyond our windshield. She could not bear to drive past any historical marker, or to cross any bridge if her book said once the Sharden Brothers ran a ferry at this spot, well known to pioneers on the Westward Trek.

In the front seat the three of them. Her husband Ray was no traveler and very early in the morning always suggested a place to stop for supper if we could only get there before dark. That summer Ceely rode between them and began to use much lipstick and each mile she placed her legs carefully on one side or the other of the gearshift lever.

I was their back-seat passenger and we were headed south. I was sent because my father telegraphed money from "that hellhole he preferred to a decent home" and because my mother believed travel was broadening. So I listened to Mrs. Herdston's lecturing tongue, but I thought only of the flamingo's infectious color, and of the great hotels anchored by the ocean's shore, in Florida.

"Jefferson, you can get out and look," Mattie would call while I was still in the back seat shuffling her boxes that fell over me whenever she stopped. "Come look if you want."

After she called I could elect to do the right thing, or I could sleep. Her schoolroom voice always put it that way and as she often said when I was in her room at school, "That's America for you."

By the time I got out of the car Mrs. Herdston would be standing on the entrance steps to some county museum, her face pressed against the windows. Mattie was shaped like a stump, one that is left in cut-over land, when there has been two years' growth of brier. Yet a white oak stump is solid there among vines, under the crow's far picket call.

A great teacher, my mother always said. That is, Mrs. Herdston told you the Right or Wrong of it. If a boy were running around until all hours of the night she would have a little talk with him, to save him from the Workhouse, or Marriage Too Young. Or she saw to it about the Army or the Navy. A little enlistment, she felt, never hurt anyone. Over the years, though, the school board tried to fire all married teachers, but she had scotched that by petitions. A few laughed because she wore the same velveteen dress the year around, but no one laughed to her face.

So we stopped where a Union spy was taken; the birthplace of an opera singer; where a regiment of Illinois Volunteers was "cut asunder by Jensen's intrepid cavalry"; and we saw the farthest reach of a cave where hollowed-out logs were used for pipes when soldiers labored in the foul air to mine saltpeter, so that other soldiers could unloose a fusillade at Indians concealed among trees.

Toward midnight they would argue and would finally decide on a motel. Then Ceely and her mother disappeared through a door into their room, and I heard two suitcases snap open. Usually Ray and I also shared the same bed, to save money. Ray would stretch his arms toward the ceiling and would say, "Day's work, wahn't it?"

If I got to sleep, the great black square trucks passed again and again inside my head, or black seals like black projectiles broke upward from the beach and the sand of my dreams.

II

The first morning I awoke at Miami Beach, they had already gone out. Mrs. Herdston was up at daylight, and saw the ocean off Collins Avenue before anyone else. Together Mattie and Ray strolled past all of the unopened shops, and saw a candy store lined entirely with red satin. By noon she was back again at our hotel. I was almost awake. She poked me in the ribs and tried to be forgiving. More than half our time in the Playland of the South was already gone, she said, and outside were new frontiers.

Above my bed the black fan blades chopped at the hot ceiling; outside a palm frond rowed in the breeze. The sun washed each stucco wall, and through the window I could see farther up the beach where the really big hotels reared into the sky, monuments erected by lovers of the sun.

So I dressed and walked outside to see the beach. The children ran crying to their mothers when the sea sucked lettuce crates and the floating husks of coconuts through the iron groins. When the children cried the women got up from the sand, the sun guards of white celluloid taped firmly like beaks across the nose. The women turned their backs to the sun and the ocean and stood there: waves bent above their coiled shell-children on the sand.

No one swam far from shore so the lifeguard dozed in his high white chair under a canvas. His hands remained crossed upon his belly of golden flesh. The dark glasses which were his eyes were sightless from his profession of watching an empty sea. And this was the beach in the afternoon.

But when the sun was down the spotlights on the walls and

in the palm trees turned everything that was not dark to silver. The upper stories of the hotels were a floating terrace of lights overhead. The cars that had been roosting under the palm fronds came out into the streets and drilled past. Inside these cars the quick puff of light from a match showed the driver's face and perhaps, also the bare shoulders of the woman beside him.

After dark I really did meet someone I knew. That's the way they say it happens. I saw her walking along the other side of the street, her head erect. I ran across the street, through traffic, and from behind, I called her name.

Ceely turned and waited. She noticed I was panting. She laughed and said she thought I fell in the ocean, and I said Fancy meeting you here, and she said Dr. Jefferson I presume, and I said The condemned man ate a hearty meal.

Ceely's blue organdy sash blew very slightly ahead of us in the breeze, so we walked off together in that direction. She wore the white opened-toed sandals. Her hair was nearly blonde from our travel. She was not really as tall as I was, though at first you might think so. As we walked she put her arm through mine. Ahead, on each side of the street, were neon lights. Inside the heavy slab-glass doors the men in burnt umber, or mauve, or turquoise dinner jackets waited near the bars, or they sat at tables farther back where the music was.

The Maritime. It's the one with nets and sponges outside, and porthole windows. The night club was like some illuminated crustacean rolled from the ocean floor, come to rest and finally secured on this street beside the ocean after a hurricane.

Inside the Club Maritime we waited in line. Through the low sea-fog smoke inside, the yellow candles burned like buoy lights along some easy summer coast; beyond the ledge of tables the dance floor was small and polished and almost concealed by the high gold satin panels above the dance band. The musicians were from the Barbados—all black, except for their girl singer.

The headwaiter leaned toward me and said softly, "Oh, you two have been waiting. That's too bad. And you two are out for a date?"

I said we thought that we would dance some.

The music began when someone from the Barbados pounded on the smallest drum. We did not hear the whole piece. We were out in the street again very quickly, walking away very fast. I could not tell Ceely that the head waiter whispered into my ear, "No tie. Gotta have a tie."

We ended up on a bench, in a small park that faced the ocean. Ahead the breakers tripped and fell, one after the other, upon the shore. Behind us the door of some hotel kitchen opened. The spear of light from the opened door came across the darkness and ticked for a moment across her face. For one frozen, light-flicked moment, I saw her face, immobile in the spear of light, staring out across the ocean.

"Not a nice walk," Ceely said, without taking her face from the ocean. I was trying to see the brighter side of things, since both of our mothers advised this.

"Damnit," she said and spat once into the sand, "I have put up with that mother of mine all through Tennessee and Georgia. We finally get where we are going. And you (Ceely turned on me) *you* don't have sense enough to wear a tie!"

I did not say anything. I had not wanted to dance, really, because I could dance only a little, and not at all to the small drums from the Barbados.

Not a nice walk for me either, but I could not say that. The car sickness came on me all over again and I thought of the automobile we had passed in Georgia, its wheels in the air, aimed at a ditch. Near the road side there was something under a bed quilt, but we did not stop. It was not a point of interest.

I sat on the bench in the cooling salt tide of air. I seemed to see us from a distance, as though I were standing nearby, staring ahead at the two figures and the organdy sash trembling in the breeze. The voice in my ear was my father's voice, and I remembered him standing on our porch, on Fancy Street, a billed cap of white duck slanted across his face. That last time I saw him he was standing beside me at the porch rail, looking out as though our dun-colored street were the wake of a ship somewhere off Penang. "How about you Jeff-boy," he said. "You getting any? Are you?" He was a merchant sailor. The next day he was gone.

As I watched it, my arm went out and around Ceely's small shoulders. I was surprised how easy it was. She seemed to lie athwart my arms, as though I had suddenly, by my touch, turned her straight small back into a length of some easy, clinging thing. When all moonlight was cut off by the clouds, I quickly kissed her.

Ceely did not stiffen in my arms and it was curious how I could tell this though I seemed, still, to be divorced from those two people on the bench in the darkness. She was yielding, as all the stories said. She put her head even closer to my shirt, and I felt her small breath very close to my skin. Because I did not know what to do, or because I was afraid, we sat there for a very long time.

After she put my hand down there she said, Oh, now we are in Florida and are on the beach . . . now. Ceely, herself, got up and took me by the hand.

Ahead was the retaining wall. The darkness of the other side would conceal us. She knew this, also, and she led me to the wall. The wall curved away under the palm trees in the darkness, and beyond was the sand, and beyond the sand the breakers tripped over themselves in the moonlight, and broke into foam.

For a moment Ceely stood on the retaining wall, facing the beach and the sea. She raised herself on tiptoe. She released my hand. I understood I was to follow. Instead I pushed her. Forward. With a little cry, Ceely leaped down. And into the shadow.

. . . Toward the Everglades, and the sky beyond the Tamiami Trail: Ray was expecting a hurricane, so we got out of the state. We saw the old fortifications at Vicksburg, and paused at Muscle Shoals where generators were buried in the deepest foundations of those dams, to fire great surges of current along the cables, to make lights burn somewhere on a farm so that a man does not have to milk in the early morning darkness in winter. It was dark and raining when we recrossed the river into Ohio and it was midnight when we drove along under the trees of the little town we had started from. At our house there was a light on the porch and my mother was up because Mrs. Herdston's cards had come through all right . . .

III

Ray married again. His next wife owned the eight-room hotel and some other property in Blanton. At 3 P.M. Ray becomes her night clerk. His health is better because of his year-around regular hours.

Ceely married. She ran off to Kentucky with a man who sold aluminum ware, house-to-house. One morning he knocked and Ceely answered the door. When the man is not on the road they live in a trailer park in El Dorado, Arkansas. Ceely, they say, did not inherit her mother's brains.

As they had planned in the beginning, the school board waited until Mrs. Herdston took off on our vacation and then they fired all married teachers. They say it killed her. They found her in bed, wearing the velveteen dress that clung to her big hips like bark around a tree stump. Perhaps all the swelling was from the years of standing on her feet, marking the Right and the Wrong of it on a hundred blackboards. Except for my mother no one ever mentions Mrs. Herdston, but as yet they have not found anyone quite like her for the job.

Just before graduation I left high school and my mother's complaints about being on her feet all day in the local bank. I made a break. I went all the way back to Miami Beach. For almost a year I worked in a hotel. I worked in the kitchen. Salads, mostly.

Going and coming from work I often stopped to look at the exact place where Ceely jumped from the retaining wall, where I pushed her down and away from me the night she took my hand and led me from the bench. The wall seemed lower now, but the night I pushed her, Ceely's face looked up once at me from the shadows, and she cried out.

Like a serpent groping in the shadow a man's pale arm encircled her knees. Her lips shaped. She screamed my name. Like some white climbing animal she tried to scramble back up the wall. I did not move. Ceely fell back again upon him. She kicked furiously at the groping arms. Before I could move or could call out or could follow, Ceely ran down the ocean side of the wall, and out of sight under the palm trees.

The man was some great crustacean, abandoned there by the tides; the waves kept us from hearing his snores. After she was gone the man sat slowly upright. He was huge in the darkness, in a muddy cook's apron, wearing his cook's white, muddy hat.

His bulged face, glazed as a bun, floated upward to my feet. His face was directly in the cleaver edge of light above the top of the wall. I thought it was whisky in his hand, but it was a square sullen bottle of lemon extract. His mouth opened. A gold cap on a tooth in the back of his throat caught the light.

"Ev-re-body," he said hoarsely. "Every-body . . . gets a dance with me. . . ."

Then the cook who was muddy turned toward the ocean. He walked with his feet wide apart, the square bottle in one hand, towards the lines of foam along the water's edge.

But the reason I came home again was this: somewhere in the North Japan Sea, at the edge of a typhoon, my father washed overboard from a tanker. Mother said I should come home and live with her on the insurance. And that is how it all came out.

Now I sit on the porch and look at the ocean-colored street and sometimes think back on the big trip to Florida, when

Mrs. Herdston's lecturing voice explained all of the points of interest.

Although I remember everything that happened very clearly, it is nothing. Nothing at all for there is no one else around who also remembers. Except perhaps Mother. She still stands on her feet all day in the bank, and she still complains at night. She works at the bank so we can both have a decent home, she says. And I cook for the two of us. Salads mostly.

An Assault in This Park

An Assault in This Park

In that moment of noon their car doors opened suddenly like metal wings: the waves ceased driving themselves upon the fatally attractive shore, and the cavalry of leaves freed at last from the molting branches charged into the grass and everything was still.

The two oldest girls squirmed themselves out of the back seat. They circled across the park and through the colonnade and around the bandstand shell where the man was running stiff-legged, drumming the turf with their heels.

While the parents got out of the car and pushed through a hole in the hedge, the baby clung to mother. This third little girl chewed upon a new pain, for unknown to any of them, or to the baby, a tooth was under the gums, already unleashing the old authority of bone over flesh. The father carried the lunch basket, very much—he thought—like what he was: a middle-class instructor, with a lower-middle-class income. Even so, he did not think the day was at all ambiguous.

Their table lay flat in the sun. Even after they had spread a teatowel for a cloth, and had spread all the tea cups and the sandwiches, the slab of stone seemed bare and primitive and much larger than either of them had thought at first.

She bent toward the ground, to the stroller, to comfort their baby. She caught her husband's face, framed for a second at eye level within the hoop of the basket handle. He was looking away, where the lake itself dog-legged out of sight. The orange flame of the leaves upon the shore seemed to draw together in the distance and become a wall. The line of blue-shadow flesh under his chin would become a jowl in only six more years. She knew they would be safely entered into middle age by then, but not before.

She had watched his face closely when he had come up the back stairs, really expecting soup. He had hesitated and had said, Why Kate, this is a *swell* idea.

Then, with a perfect statement that showed how little he realized her central importance in this dense household routine,

—How *did* they all get dressed at once?

So much was demanded of her, and if she resisted there was a price. She had worked to break down what she thought was a "fatal reserve" between them, and the "real intimacy" she got was the perfect contempt he could display for a hasty lunch, never realizing she had been furiously engaged with their babies all morning. For the children, there was another price. At this new school the childless women with Ph.D.'s, or the women with "planned" families of one lucky boy-child, were bitches about "one's independent interests." This independence, she thought, was a contradiction; she read most of the books Harry read—and more too. It infuriated her to be known, categorically, as a "fine little manager."

From all the possibilities she saw in life, she had wanted children. The University was dull but she felt, vaguely, the children would profit in some way. Age, age, was upon her. It was death she feared, for she was acutely aware that one molar was decaying while she slept. The colic hours of mid-night hung the funeral-wreath circles under her eyes. Her skin was wrinkling slightly, and Harry would soon notice this, perhaps tomorrow.

Therefore she lived in a cyclic state of withdrawal and return in her affection for Them and for Self. Her phases were either a sunshine street, or the dark, withdrawn, bedroom afternoons when she could neither work nor sleep. This day she had wanted to leave their apartment near the University for the park, the sun, and the stone slab. The long Finger Lake was passive and fecund before her.

A college couple, the girl in freshly cleaned saddle shoes, the boy in a purple Windbreaker, walked along the margin of the lake. They did not see the lunch spread upon the stone table nor did they hear the discord of the university bells which escaped across water and vanished.

—The packet of contraceptives: she had found them in his toolbox, in the car. And her wrinkles. Was she . . .?

She watched those walkers of the beach and felt protective toward them. She would offer them a piece of cake, but there was not enough for that. She could still believe they were not hungry.

Across the park some Italians were seated around a long wooden table, smiling over ripe olives and the wine. There was a roasted turkey in the center of their checkered cloth. On the grass the accordion carelessly flowed in red bellows out of the purple-lined instrument case. One of the men wore a soldier's suit, but if he were going into the army, or returning home alive, she could not tell.

The man in the bandstand shell was still poised upon the railing, head bent, staring at the floor. The little girls came drumming toward her, through a spray of leaves.

—Oh Harry, isn't it simply a perfect day? I'm so glad you wanted to come.

He turned from his scrutiny of the lake; he would like to slash through those waves sometime, in a power boat. He had been considering, while he sat on top of the stone slab, about these narrow shores which seemed to come to a point, around which no eye could see. He turned his face to her lunch spread on the table.

—You have good ideas, Kate, he said jovially. And we got Romance, too.

He winked and pointed his ferule nose at the young couple walking the shore, hand in hand.

He opened the thermos of tea and poured his own cup full. The two eldest girls snatched their sandwiches and ran toward the bandstand. He did not call after them because he did not want to shout in public. But they went only a little way toward the man who seemed to be sunning himself. They sat down abruptly. They nibbled the white bread, pecking as birds do, chattering something.

Well, they were growing up. He dreaded this, and their possibilities worried him: Sarah was dark, verbal. She had already used the word "co-operation" and had dismayed him by this portent. Elsie was soft and yielding, an easily fractured child that nuzzled a blanket all night and all day. The baby seemed, as yet, no type at all. Even so, it enraged him when clucking women said, she looks *exactly* like *you*.

He thought he knew how unhappy women could be—he'd made a few so himself. He realized, now, he had been destructive. He knew exactly how to seduce the brilliant dark, Sarah ones: with ideas that lead to . . . well, as far as a man wanted to go. Then there had been all those easy soft Elsie-women, who never asked for anything but a chance to be seen in public, in a soft loose dress . . . Ah, *descheveler*, and early sorrow. . . .

Sorrow or the Woman's Foreign Legion, as he called nursing, or the Law. Or perhaps they would make an early, abrupt alliance with a Union Man, a welder. He tried not to think of these things—he knew it was silly. Still, each week, they grew. The idea of them being committed to what he'd been through was too much; so he thought of something else.

If he were successful everything would be different. Here in the East he saw how important the right schools were, especially when children were young. Perhaps he could educate them "at home," could send them off on scholarships because they knew their Latin, their Old French. The idea of making them prodigies, of putting them into a fancy school, without any money, repelled him. He loved them too much to make them in his own image: unhappy.

That morning, however, he had met his class. Miss Bunny Emerson giggled at the question of ambiguity, "And he said saddle me the ass, and he saddled him."

The referent, Miss Emerson, to "him"?

She was silent. At that moment he saw them all. Four of them not prepared; six frankly not interested ("What's ambiguity, sir?"); Mr. Schirol and Mr. Schudil and Mr. Riefling were still thinking of the ROTC drill floor, wondering whether to apply now for flight training, and hit Korea in jets next year, or . . . *It's the way the ball bounces* . . .

—*What* is the referent of "him," Mr. Kann?

Mr. Kann was not asleep, but the presence of tomorrow's football game was already here, like a wet jersey in the corner of a locker room. This damp inertia was also in the minds of his colleagues: a wet jersey in the corner. Oh, to think of the professorial ranks, those with tenure: men who wore flannel slacks, and iron-gray hair; men who had once been students of much promise, who had "done their work" under Smart, or Sweet, or even Kittredge. They were in the image of those righteous, bearded masters who had been honestly repelled by the business world, who had been nevertheless bold and predatory in the matter of departmental politics, robber barons of the mind. Their "students of promise," to-day's professors, still pursued "research," their philosopher's stone. They were merely gluttons upon the footnote.

He resented them. They were not teachers. Therefore he liked to say, loudly, in their presence, "A *dull* teacher is intolerable, y'know." Nor did he consider they might silently concur, and thus return his compliment. But they did say aloud, "Old Robbie dull? Thorough, rather, one *should* say."

He knew, however, his gadfly criticism directed at their old masters was a pose. He envied their rank—and salary. He envied their seminars of one student: feather-bedding, he told his fellow instructors. The other instructors repeated it. The place was a nest of gossip, no real Democracy of the mind; a good teacher was not valued or rewarded or recognized. So he ended the class, abruptly:

—All right! Suppose you think about that for next time. The referent to "him."

He closed his book and went up to his office where the tea water was just beginning to boil. There would be no conferences because the lights were turned off, so he back trailed through the landscape of all his errors: the war, and how he could have avoided the draft—could have been commissioned, perhaps in the Navy; should have known about the Air Force where he would have been a Warrant Officer, at least. And *that* would have given him money for an Eastern University. He should have been a "student of promise." A letter would have gone along with his PMLA article . . . "Enclosed piece is by a very promising student of mine . . . I think it *very* interesting, William. 'Course it's more in your field, than mine. . . ." Or should he have gone to college at all? But he had gone, and here he was.

He sat in the office, letting the tea get cold in his hand. He realized he would teach Freshman English for years; he wasn't exactly a favorite. There were other, younger instructors who had really completed the thesis.

He made the decision once again: stand or fall as a *teacher*. After all, they were also needed. On the desk were two sets of single paragraphs (the Department had given up on themes). A few nervous people in the class had already inquired about these back papers. He removed his glasses and polished the lenses, as though breathing on glass would cure, forever, his fluttering optic nerve. Someone knocked, but he was just stepping out to lunch.

On the way home to their apartment he had driven the long way down the hill. He'd have to face more questions about the opened package of contraceptives.

He'd bought them, but why? It was innocent enough:

when they had been in the jungle in the Army you always waterproofed everything in rubbers. It was efficient, a joke, and it kept off rust and mold. Recently he'd protected the car tools and flashlight in this same way.

But she had found the opened box when she looked for a screw driver. No explanation satisfied her. She said it was because she was old and ugly, made so by *his* children. Yet her outburst made him face his own motive: had he really hidden them, "Just in God-damned case of emergency?"

He had been unable to answer when she pointed out, after all, this University was *not* the jungles.

Lately he had felt a predatory restlessness creep like a vine over him: he had asked a waitress, almost casually, what record she would hear on the jukebox. She had said, "I'll Dance at Your Wedding," so he played it. Her name was Doris; she had just "gra-du-ated from h'school." He had thought, but he had not said, do you do baby-sitting, too? Instead he had only walked out and she had giggled at him over her cash register.

He was through with all of that. Yet other things could upset him: the invitations to fraternity houses, where the older successful alumni often dropped in. He knew that kind. He felt very discreet for never having told her all his Army experiences. He had censored some things about the dark steamy jungle and what went on under the ferns with the old gang of the Medical Detachment. That was all over, too.

He walked up their back stairs, and had seen the picnic basket. He would have preferred lunch to be absolutely on the table, but in a second he accepted the idea of eating in the park.

Even after they had driven out to the lake he did not think this little trip had been considerable trouble for her. As he turned his head from the lake, he looked down through the hoop of their basket handle and watched her lifting their crying baby from the stroller.

—Oh I don't know what's the matter, she said; the poor little thing.

—Maybe it's the wind, giving her colic, he told her. But there was so little conviction in his voice she did not reply.

The couple on the beach were now past. Across the park in the colonnade he heard the Italian man in the soldier suit playing the accordion. This music and the percussion of clapped hands echoed through the park.

Suddenly with an abandon she had not seen for a long time, he stood up on their stone table, hopped up and down like a rooster, then leaped lightly to the ground. He ran quickly through the leaves and around the colonnade toward his girls.

He found them by the swings. They were all together.

She had brought the baby, on her hip. The older girls got into the swings, laughing as he pushed them higher, "*upso high. Touchthesky!*"

Now there were others in the park: nursemaids, with one child; men not on shift; high school students skipping band practice; the friends of the Italian, who was now playing the scales. People with bread, come to feed the tame mallards. These people wandered in and out of the colonnade, or turned to stare across the lake.

Suddenly everyone heard the speaker.

In a single motion of attention, each face turned toward the bandstand shell. The man who had been withdrawn, his head bent in communion with himself, or in a trance, was being introduced. He was being introduced to no one at all.

But the introduction began. Therefore the Italians ceased to clap their hands, the men off-shift from the chain factory turned and shuffled through the leaves. Some were already attentive.

She clutched Harry's arm. Something was dangerous. She felt the picnic was over; she wanted to suggest he go back to his office. But he wanted to listen; something here invited his criticism. He turned to listen out of brute curiosity.

At the edge of the bandstand were "helpers." They appeared from somewhere. They were the people on Saturday street corners. They wore factory-cut suits. They drove old cars, decorated with much chrome and foxtails, with a "Meet Jesus" tag on the license plates. They were machinists and cat-skinners and air-hammer men who sold the *Watch Tower* on week-end corners. They formed a cordon around the bandstand shell, waiting for the main speaker.

The introducer wiped his face with a bandanna. He slipped a raw stick of Juicy Fruit chewing gum into his mouth. He sat erect, as though he had done his job well.

The real speaker did not stir from his position of meditation. His face was withdrawn from the crowd. Then he stood up, his arms like sticks at his side:

"Now I won't detain you folks long this day Oh no, not long this day, this long *long* day . . ."

The *Watch Tower* people said *a*-men (God-damn) *a-men!* They were captive, intent.

The speaker was very tall, when he drew up his chin. His voice was shrill, like a woman's. His only gesture as he spoke was the long whiplash finger, pointing at them from the railing of the bandstand. The finger darted out as though it were alive, on a dead hand. The finger would quiver, droop, or writhe. On the finger the sun caught the huge zircon ring, blinded those who looked.

He wore a battle jacket, but there were square-headed, chromium rivets for the rank and insignia. From the shoulder straps purple and red and orange ribbons fluttered. When the breeze blew the ribbons whipped across his mouth so that he spoke and breathed through a bundle of writhing color. The jacket was crudely sewed with wire to the lower half of zippered coveralls. The pockets bulged with papers. The shrill voice sawed the wind, and they could see only the zircon's pot of light, or themselves, reflected in the fanatical luster of his shoes.

"Oh, my fellow citizens. Let there be among you certain Ones of Cleanliness: you are clean, or you are not. There is no compromise. Denounce them, therefore, who are not *clean*. Disfellowship those of the tribe of Pharisee. Let the

purest disfellowship the Pretenders, by the swift wing and
sword of his *Will!*"

She heard this and held firmly to Harry's arm, as though
she had found protection. He felt her hand and smiled and
said audibly, No doubt he will haul out the Bible next, and
the Constitution.

The speaker fixed the cordon of Witnesses with his finger.
He unsnapped a pocket of the trousers and took out a worn
pamphlet. He began to read, his voice becoming more and
more shrill in the rising wind. The audience stayed, almost
against their will. The Cordon of *Watch Towers* chanted, *A*-
men (hot damn) A-*men!*

"It is *He* who will be among you. *He* is now a Captain.
And with him I fought in Korea. The Reds shall not stand
before him! His old Platoon shall assemble upon this shore.
He will speak of *order* and cleanliness and of the tribes which
shall inherit our Native Land. And you shall assemble to hear
him in this selfsame park when his battle is over over there.
I say unto you . . ."

Rain drops on the branches and on the dry leaves and on
their own heads aroused them. The audience, except for the
cordon around the speaker, turned away to protect their
properties. The nursemaids ran, lumbering and squealing
toward the babies who were alone and unprotected under the
leafless branches of trees.

She was glad of the rain. She did not know what this shrill
violent speech was about—a man who was unbalanced probably. Even though there were authorities to take care of such
cases, she thought of sex crimes, of the apartment, and of the
little girls. She was glad to leave, and yet the "speech" amused
Harry, had made her party a success.

—Sounded like the real thing, didn't it?

They had turned away from the bandstand shell. They expected the girls to run on ahead. But the parents were talking
as they walked toward their car. They really did not notice,
for a second.

The cordon was still standing at attention.

On the steps of the bandstand shell, also transfixed, reaching from the very top step toward the shoes, was Elsie: blonde, soft, yielding, at the top of the stairs. She was gazing intently at the speaker. If he noticed her, he said nothing. He stared at the floor, looking at the boards beneath his articulate shoes. Elsie's hand went out once more, reaching for the shoes.

Sarah, so verbal, yet shy, stood apart. She did not climb the stairs, nor did she appear to retreat. So she stood in the limbo of indecision, facing the speaker, unable to leave, yet pawing the turf with the toe of her shoe.

Harry ran back. He carried away one girl under each arm.

He did not put them on the ground until they were through the colonnade, and back at their stone-topped table.

He was ready to beat them with a switch.

But she said, Why Harry! They only wanted to see. After all they are not adults!

He felt they were too willing to be taken in by fools.

The little girls ran to the car. They climbed into their back seat and asked for the bottles of milk which their mother had brought along.

They went home again. They carried the children upstairs to their cribs. The afternoon nap received them. They slept, without knowing the rain was beginning to fall. Only the baby was restless, for the tooth beneath the gums was relentless.

She felt this had been a real family outing; she knew he enjoyed it as much as he *could* enjoy anything; she understood this about him, that he was incapable of being happy without some reserve or qualification; but this day he had been nearly so. She would not even think further about the contraceptives. He did silly things; everyone did. She forgave him, in her own mind, and did completely forget her own hurt.

He was anxious to be away from this apartment. There was work at the office, the paragraphs. He kissed her lightly on the ear, and walked whistling downstairs, and out through the rain to the car.

On the road to the high raining atmosphere of the University he thought it was good to get out in the open; being with Kate and the girls seemed, indeed, to help him get through each day. He wished he could abandon himself, could accept them for what they were, without trying to legislate them into adulthood too soon.

As he drove up the hill, where the rain drops were larger, more disciplined; he wondered what that shrill gathering could mean, if anything. Was it some new order, slipping into the frayed edge of this town; would they enter, finally, into the corridors of Gustave-Schmidt Hall, new barbarians among the plaster casts of Venus and Niobe? Some New Beast, infiltering Jerusalem, to be born.

He searched for a parking place. He turned over in his mind once again the possibilities of leaving this department, and this school, and this town for at least one year: on a Guggenheim, or a Fulbright, or on a Ford Foundation grant. And who else better deserved it?

From a year's leave would come the Book; perhaps a better job. There would be scholarships for all the girls, in some adequate Eastern school. After he raised them, of course.

The Claims Artist

The Claims Artist

Three hours' pay was all he had coming the first morning on the museum job, when the Ready-Mix truck backed toward the forms of the retaining wall. The dual wheels rocked deep into the trembling clay he had just shoveled out of the trench. He stood by the truck to place the tip of the cement chute into the form and the braced reinforcing steel. It tickled him to see how nicely phallic all this was. He thought, as he rested his hand on the Ready-Mix trough, of Form and Content, the essence of literary endeavor.

Bring her back, more!

The truck driver's boot slipped off the clutch. The truck jerked. The chute buckled, a giant shears.

Hold it! was all he heard the foreman yell from somewhere high above, in the girders.

He did not scream until on the clay by his shoe he saw the class ring, with his own finger still through it.

They took him away in a city ambulance. As he climbed into the back, holding his own tourniquet, he saw a clerk changing the sign above the timekeeper's shack to read, "Zero Days Without an Accident."

Oh there had been—what he thought then—meaningless hospital forms to fill out. At Admissions he told them no, he had no Blue, or Red, or White Cross. He was by profession? A, ahhh, put down laborer. Finally they wheeled him into surgery.

That night he was back where he had started, when he had decided to work at least a few days. It was a furnished room and he shared the toilet with a huge woman who wore only a corset while she frizzed her hair, standing with her legs like that. She was too old or careless to lock the bathroom from the inside so he often surprised her, but she always said only, "Hey!"

He had known a job of actual labor would come out badly. But it was so damned hard, he thought as he sat in the chair where he read *The Counterfeiters* over and over. The necessity for independence was the hawk within him—beaked, austere, alone—visible only in the compulsive way he talked and blew out cigarette smoke at the same time, or in his nervous eye, dark as a gambler's. He was the last receptacle of his family line—had not seen them since the war—and he held in a kind of trust the thing that had made all of them brawlers at schoolboard meetings, the ones who would assault any deputy, the tobacco chewers in the center of any county meeting who would stomp a boot or interrupt a Farmer's-Week Republican by shouting, *By God, no ye don't say it; by Dammy, she ain't a fact!* And then someone would throw the first chair.

From that line of sour-land farmers, and jackleg lawyers who owned the swamplands fit only for sheep (if their hoofs didn't rot off), he got this brute love of isolation that kept him whole in the city. And from them, too, he got his mean, hickory-root manners that made no one at all care for him. In fact, he went out mostly at night, when the city seemed more like a grove of oaks.

In this way he kept their honesty—and their cussedness—alive, even though they had long forgotten about him. If something was published, or if someone promised to publish, or if they even praised him, he would get drunk that night. In this way he was like his forefathers, who for no reason at all would fight and run through fields all night, wild on jug whisky. And like them he never slept late but was always up promptly at six, or whenever the first light came into the alley on which his window faced.

Even so he never considered whether what he wrote was worthwhile: he was too proud to think of this, and too irascible to think about money, though he always took whatever he could get. He lived however he could: first on the G.I. bill, the 52/20 club, unemployment benefits, VA Insurance Refunds, and once off a woman. But the woman had interfered with his work, and he had determined never to do it again. After all the money had been parceled out for milk and Corn Flakes and boxes of raisins and typewriter ribbons and hell's own amount of first-class postage, he had taken the laboring job. He had lied about his experience, though he seemed to talk more like a laborer than the foreman.

He went to bed, then, fully expecting to live as he had always lived, but without a few of the fingers on his left hand.

The next morning, when the odor of frizzed hair was especially annoying in the furnished room, the agents knocked at the door. He was not shaved and was wearing his old bathrobe. The two men from the Compensation Bureau merely shoved the empty beer cans off the settee and made themselves at home. After they saw how large the roaches were, however, they sat more lightly upon the bulging settee, afraid of what they might squeeze from it.

One of the administrators, it seemed, was from Diagnosis; the other was Compensation. They worked as a team, and this wouldn't take a minute.

They brought out the X-ray negatives and the large box and placed these things on the rug among the loose chapters of the manuscript of the novel.

"Now you see," Diagnosis said, "you are deprived, through employer neglect, right *through here*." He drew a black line on the large plaster cast of the hand inside the box.

The writer looked from his bandages to the plaster cast. He said nothing for he expected nothing from people of this kind. He disliked them simply because they were what they were—"the team."

"Now y'see," Compensation said, "this calls for two hundred and sixty dollars—without occupational calamity. The sixty is for the half-finger, y'see?"

But I can't type now! The writer sulked, growled. He was angry because he did not realize the huge amount of money they had mentioned. Besides, he didn't like for people to stay longer than was necessary.

The two men from the state office looked at each other and at the novels in stacks, almost to the ceiling. The old refrigerator was still trying to pound cold into the ice trays, but its own heat undid the work and only the outside edges of the cubes could freeze. The odor of frizzed hair submerged them. This case was certainly—and they thought this corporately—certainly in the nature of occupational calamity.

The next day the check for $500 arrived. When he saw this fine amount he laughed and laughed. He lay down on the settee and talked to this new friend, this beautiful bandaged hand. Finally the woman in the bathroom stuck her head through the door and pointed her curling iron at him and yelled, "Hey!"

After this day his left hand did not hurt him at all, or if so he did not admit the pain.

In five months the money was all gone—as he knew it would be. This was good, he felt, for during that time he had not once left the furnished room, nor had he made a single unnecessary movement—like cleaning up the place, or anything like that.

The big woman had set milk and Corn Flakes inside his room, or on the toilet seat. He scarcely knew where the time had gone. He was thinner, but he had finished the novel: his prose style was more terse, resilient as a taproot. The secretaries of the publishers praised this ending, wanted to see something "like the last very fine section."

This praise made his isolation and the loss of the fingers really nothing at all, for at last he felt he was on the right track. True, he felt uneasy about having anything at all to do with the Compensation people, but he saw clearly enough a man had to live and to do his work some way. Though he distrusted them, and laughed at them, they were useful; beyond that he was not capable of thinking. In fact, he never could really think, and was apt to be very foolish when he did. He was only worth a damn, he often said to the frizzed-haired woman who now stood occasionally with her head through the door, "I'm not wuff a damn, unless I'm right at this desk."

The morning after he had lived out the money, he walked to the airport. It was not far away; he had heard motors warming up, early in the morning. It was the private field nearest the city where the industrialists and doctors parked their ships. The airplanes, wingtip to wingtip, in the morning sun like a row of aristocratic silver and yellow birds, excited him. They suggested flight and travel, two things that he often thought of but had never actually done on his own.

The crew chief hired him at once. "Just wash them," he said, and tossed out a pair of white coveralls.

The writer entered once more into the world beyond the furnished room, and the alley, and the odor of frizzed hair. He was in sunlight, on the line, dousing the metal wings furiously with buckets of detergent. He enjoyed this water play. And he thought, as he kept his eye peeled for an incoming ship, certainly a fiction is like this airplane: a word structure that is balanced, braced, and designed in a form organic to its function. And the reader's eye assaults this structure as the water from the hose assaults this metal skin. And rereading, you might say, merely shines a fiction. This analogy would have to be thought out, but he completely rejected his older idea of Form and Content.

A blue and white Navion rolled imperiously to the gas pit on the apron. He dropped the hose and ran out in front of the hangar. The pilot was a traveling agent for the Eagles

Lodge, traveling with his wife from Pittsburgh to a Cleveland Aerie. He presented his Credit Card and got back in the airplane.

After he started the engine, he motioned, *Come here a minute*. The writer, at the moment, was standing just in front of the leading edge of the wing. The man asked, which way is this traffic pattern?

Without the slightest hesitation the writer took one step toward the nose of the plane. He pointed directly ahead, through the slicing prop.

He awoke in the hospital. The crew chief had left him there. Because the writer was a new man at the field, no one thought about a tourniquet, already in place just below the shoulder when they got to him. Later someone took away the arm. In a basket.

This time he was much longer in the hospital, but he kept pestering the nurses to let him go home to work. The Compensation team made their visit, as he figured they would. Now he had enough to last eighteen months.

The big woman heard him enter: she had cleaned up everything (all those old papers) while he was gone. He was so glad to see her that he did not mention the half a novel she had swept from the floor and burned. Besides, he felt it was not his best work. She looked at the sleeve pinned ostentatiously across his breast and said, "*Hey*," with a certain amount of tenderness.

He found he did not need more than four hours' sleep, and now he could not write novels. They made him sick. He could write only the short story. These short forms were more intense than anything else he had ever done. In fact they were nearly poetic, and only the nonpaying literary quarterlies would accept them, "for future publication, but in what distant future issue can now not at all be ascertained because of finances . . . in the meantime, send us more of what you do!"

The huge woman now came in every night, picked up the manuscripts for him, and put them in the order he directed.

She also helped do the small jobs that required two hands: tying the shoestrings, buttoning the top button on a shirt collar. In fact, by unspoken agreement and what he thought was pity on her part, the door between their rooms remained open so only the toilet and the bathtub was between them.

He was happy because he worked all day and all night, the typewriter table swaying under the assault of his good right hand. The stories became shorter, he noticed. It was impossible for him to write a sentence of more than one independent clause. Ideas for new short stories came at him as he worked, and he simply stopped between paragraphs to record them in code on the wallpaper over his desk. Finally the wall and all the walls were covered with germinating stories, some with mouths clamoring to be written.

Each week brought the rejections. Each week he revised and the big woman sent them back out. If there were an acceptance, (and there were many) she would pick it out of the piled envelopes and the wheedling notes from literary agents and would say, *Hey!*

It was then that he began to send her out for rich food. He was not a Corn Flake man any more. She brought in paper cartons of mashed potatoes and fine beef gravy; fried shrimp, lobster tails, and grocery bags full of canned salmon, *paté*, and soda crackers. She opened these cans and arranged them before him.

He would taste, judiciously, then lose control and begin to gobble everything at once while he talked. When he was finished, he threw the cartons and the sacks and the tin cans into the corner and began to work once more.

Once a literary agent from New York found his way up the alley and peered in the window.

This man wore California open-toed sandals and sunglasses with blue lenses. He did not like what he saw inside the room: the stacks of books, the untidy manuscripts, and the body stretched out on the grimy and lumpy settee. So he got back on the bus and went on to Steubenville, where a woman was getting together a new series of books, *Casserole Cookery, for Your Fireplace*.

At this moment, the writer was not asleep. He was again considering Literary Theory, the matter of the versification of a poem. Clearly there were two categories involved: the effect from devices such as meters, and stanza groupings. And secondly, there was the reader's total comprehension, after which one worked back through the poem, upon the *expectation* that Class One items *would* be a unified psychological experience. Consequently, Poetry was largely based in Hope. And there the speculation ended though he now could not sleep because of excitement.

The next day the big woman accosted him: nothing for breakfast. She presented him with the empty cookie tin where the money always was, and she gave him, also, a quiet rent notice and said firmly, *Hey? Hey?*

He saw for the first time the implication of what it was to be a writer, a really independent, nonkept, nonacademic, non-Hollywood, writer. Before he had seen these "accidents" simply as a joke on Diagnosis and Compensation.

He dug out the pamphlet they had sent him, and the other pamphlets that had been sent to him, as a matter of routine from all the other states in the Union. The Eye was listed in Ohio for five thousand dollars and both eyes to ten thousand dollars. In Utah it was not nearly so much. But in New York . . . He saw that the other states were practically inviting his residence. On the back page of one of the pamphlets he found what seemed to be his own portrait: the exploded diagram of a man, sectioned up into all the pieces that one could possibly lose, and still remain alive. The picture was like the charts of the best cuts of cattle and sheep which hang around the classroom walls of a Home Economics Department in a State Ag School.

By noon he got up from the couch.

He said "So long" to the huge woman and headed for the freight yards.

They would need a watchman, a one-armed night watchman for a place where all the wheels were.

The *Côte d'Azur* was supine and glistening at noon, the green line along the green shore shimmering only a little in the sparkling height of summer near St. Raphael, the poor man's Riviera. Two Americans who had been there all season, lolling in the sand, smoking cheroots, were stretching at noon for the regular lunch hour.

They both looked up—heard the music.

They absolutely opened their eyes to see what this crystalline song could be. It was words, clearly, some piping lyric, continuous.

A huge woman in a flowered silk skirt and an orange turban carried on her head, lightly as an African on safari, a basket of woven silver. She walked between the two Americans, and paused for the Portuguese lads who were cavorting on the beach, looking for cigar butts.

Hey! Hey! she honked at them, *Suieeee!*

One American put down his novel (Costain's *The Silver Chalice*) to stare after the huge woman.

Now Ralphie, do y'see that basket?

The other broker turned his head from the sun and looked at the huge woman as she steamed down the beach. He had not heard the question, so he said, "What ever happened to Fats Stockler, anyhow?"

"Why he's in Palm Beach, he's got the bad heart. I liked him, y'know. Who was that little woman he . . ."

They couldn't remember.

"That basket I mentioned. He's the Great Handicapped Poet."

"Oh *that's* him."

Sure, they ran it in Life. *Born that way. They're making a movie out of him. He plays the lead—entirely in the basket. He sings the sound track.*

The other man turned his belly to the sun and began to read Paul Bowles's *Let It Come Down.*

In a moment he closed the book and looked up, "You say, *entirely* in a basket?"

"Yes, I said in a basket. Great poet, born that way. He doesn't have any ears, even. He sings the lyrics, all the time."

"Well I'll be damned."

"Say, wasn't Fats's girl named Judy, or something?"

But they couldn't remember.

A Try from the Gulf

A Try from the Gulf

Finally he had made it to Havana where limestone columns along Malecon rear like cliffs, as though a façade of stone could influence the tide and frontier of the sea. But after the first six months he no longer sat on the sea wall, staring at Morro Castle where the police trained; nor did he loiter by the stringed music of the yacht club, where the doorman was. All of that seemed too expensive, so he dreamed of food and of fleshy billboard women. He took coffee only each morning in some dirty closed-in restaurant where at least there was a corner at one's back.

Rhave could bribe the Cuban police sergeants for a long time, though the original "passport" had improved with normal use—official stamps, and so on. Even Rhave could be trusted only a little on the problem of entry; the little toothache of uncertainty came to his mind whenever the sirens blew for noon, or when two policemen barged along a narrow street and forced him into the nearest doorway.

Like all the others who were this close to a Promised Land, such as only the homeless can imagine, he became a watcher

of boats: at the P and O Docks, later at the outgoing *goletas*
with crewmen named José and Jean who could put a man
ashore at Marathon Key. After all the boats refused him, he
hung around the Sevilla-Biltmore, but a whirlwind romance
and marriage was impossible: American schoolteachers travel
in pairs. Or it was his suit: secondhand in Grenoble, patched
by reweaving in Marseilles; lately, he had borrowed a pair of
dungarees from a clothesline. Each day he read the Miami
papers—kept them in a stack beside his bed or sold them
again—and in each notice of a real estate transfer, he saw Big
Opportunity. Sunday he read the bathing beauties, standing
against a palm tree or smiling as they bend over like that,
above the sand.

Besides it was possible: certain faces disappeared from
Parque Central, and from the Chinese barrios. By sea or by
illegal aircraft, they arrived in Jersey City where their sponsors allowed them to slave out the seven hundred dollars over
hot dishwater. Except he was not Chinese. He scarcely knew
what he was any more: some Spanish he spoke, yes. Or,
danke, danke! as he had learned quickly enough when he began to drive for the *Oberscharfuer*. Lately, however, even a
woman could not lure him to speak his mother tongue. They
always asked him about the teeth in front which were missing, about his leg that had been broken across a curb. (He had
nearly gotten away from the Partisans about the time the
Germans left.) Oh, there were ways out of a country if you
used a friend. He knew all about that. . . .

It was ten o'clock and the restaurant was in shadows. He
was balancing the *café solo* exactly at the level of his throat
when the Flyer walked in. Behind, bowing, already sweating
through the yellowed linen coat, stumbling like a regular
businessman with an important client was that ox, Señor
Rhave.

The regular Europeans in Polaco town had said, Ah yes—
a Flyer *is* here. With airplane. Consequently he had quickly
deserted them and had gone to awaken Señor Rhave . . . had
showed him the roll of American bills once again.

The Flyer stretched his feet out beyond the other side of Rhave's table. Yawned.

The waiter took away the demitasse, brought on the American coffee. This was the pilot who would take his chances with the Border Patrol: he had tiny squeezed features, mouth and nose too small for a man. No doubt he could fly well enough: the chino pants, the scarf red at the throat, the shrill girlish laughter when Rhave leaned over and said something, probably about money. . . .

"Ah shorely will, Old Hoss. Ah shorely will. . . ." The throat and the small button chin exposed to the light of the sun for only a laughing second. Then he was calling for another pitcher of water.

Rhave had looked at the money last night. Rhave had counted it the day before yesterday, in the morning. Therefore Rhave nodded once behind the Flyer's back: yes.

That was enough for a man who had waited three years, so he slipped all the sugar cubes into his pocket and went home to pack.

As he turned in the alley and through the portal of the wall, he knew he would make it this time. He deserved to, of course, for who else in all Havana had really made a study of entry.

How do you find out, without real effort, that the Border people have only one airplane, and so few men? Amateurs, really, when you thought of the fine European police. Where else—(not Canada)—would you find such dominoes as the Cuban officers? Petty grafters, stealers of fruit, free taxi riders: but one must know their methods, of course.

He was surprised when everything he owned fitted into such a small bundle. Well, he had learned all the lessons: have no friends, write no letters, attend no meetings; avoid night clubs, movies, speak only when spoken to, then leave first.

How many in Paris alone had been picked up . . . fools sticking with their wives, to be sure.

He was stretched on the iron cot in the room he occupied under a stairs, when Rhave stooped through the door, stood looking down, clearly offended by the smell of this place. Rhave would not have to say anything: Rhave would know everything was O.K. No need to say, keep off the streets: for certain bring the money. . . . Yes, he would bring the money to the airplane. Not before, no! Not a cent tonight. Thief!

Might not the weather or that so-called pilot go sour? Rhave shrugged and said don't yell about it, and then told him quietly where the car would be.

Rhave looked down at the skinny dark man on the cot. He liked much better to work with the Chinese. They kept very quiet. They sat together bravely, all in a line very much like little teams of acrobats. But Czlau was always talking about his education—had it not been for the war. Well, they all had a version of the past but this one seemed unduly interested in horses and the big tracks in Miami.

Rhave walked out through the court to the street, glad to be away from this one who had that kind of picture right up on the wall.

II

In all Havana there are many streets, and high walls, and rooms behind them: there are many desks and many dark men of "business" who arrive only very late in the evening, and who live only at hotels where any name will do, for a photo-stated hotel register can be admitted in evidence. They may have a car or a woman or a habit of some kind to support; these men do not want to go any place, personally, but if a *goleta* should head for Marathon Key, and if they can inform the Office in Miami. . . . There was Grippa, who booked passages and informed Miami at the same time. He was killed by Santos. Or there was the Ensign who put aliens ashore and said that a road, just inland, led to a great city. But the Ensign's road was only a path into the Everglades, where the quicksands were, where saw grass nearly always covered the bones.

III

Before dawn, far out across the field, in the trees at the end of the old runway the Flyer was already waiting. The dew was on the wings, and as the headlights caught him he was reaching up over the leading edge with his rolled-up coat, trying to dry off the fabric a little.

"Need all the lift," the Flyer told Rhave as they stood beside the upraised cowling, waiting for the moon to come up a little more. That afternoon the pilot had walked over the long level field, this pasture, kicking the turf. He would aim between the trees at the end of the field, then two miles mostly downhill to the ocean.

"We got twenty-three minutes," and the Flyer motioned Czlau to take one of the coats off the Chinese and rub down the wings also.

The Flyer showed him the cockpit and how to hold down the toe brakes.

Finally the pilot pulled the propeller through a few times and called, "Switch On": then he stuck his head inside the cockpit to check before he swung the wet, metal prop again. The motor caught, ran bravely among the *cibre* trees, but it seemed only a toy unwinding in the darkness.

"Load 'em," the Flyer said to everybody at once. Czlau motioned to the Chinese. They lined up at the door of the plane, neither afraid nor wanting to be the first to enter. The last Chinese had to lie across the other three who were stuffed in the baggage compartment: his face was pressed against the plexiglass, his knees trussed under his stomach. Czlau claimed the seat because he had paid Rhave and Rhave had paid the Flyer beside the plane after the engine started. Someone else would pay for the Chinese. The sponsors well knew how quickly a shark can eat a Paid-for Man, or swamps consume him.

The Flyer turned in the semidarkness of the cockpit to wave good-by to Rhave, but the automobile had already left, his lights not visible through the trees. Rhave wanted to be far from the crash scene.

Because he had not flown before, Czlau did not know when they left the ground. The top wire of the fence drifted under the wheels, the trees were only an instant beside them. The terrain dropped away ever so slightly and they remained suspended. The line of the waves on the sand were white and then they were only a little above the sea.

"You just don't know how much an egg beater like this will *lift*," the Flyer told him. "We might make it. We just might."

While they were suspended behind the propeller's steady work, Czlau thought again how clever: a light plane! No need to land at a large airport. They had no instruments really, except a compass; you could not miss the whole state of Florida. And who would believe anyone would risk it over water in this plane? Oh, it was worth the chance and the five hundred, or seven hundred if you were Chinese.

He did not know where they refueled, but the gas cans were in the bushes at dawn. The Chinese in the baggage compartment stirred when the wheels touched the ground, but they did not try to get out.

The sun was up when the city emerged before them from the flat, swampy land: below, a race track, and much farther away the white hotels, the windows already sparkling in the morning. He stared out the windshield, wanted to cruise about at housetop level, to assert himself, to celebrate a little.

But the Flyer banked cautiously as though the overloaded plane and the quivering fabric would skid out of the air. He flew it—did not glide—flew into the white, coral, abandoned highway beside a hedge.

IV

The pilot did not motion or speak. He opened the door and the Chinese unfolded, fell kneeling to the packed coral of the road. Their legs had cramped in the cold. Czlau drove them into the bushes and nodded, Yes, to the pilot. They would wait until the car honked.

Actually, the small yellow airplane had scarcely stopped rolling for them to get out: it taxied away quickly, tail high, then pulled up sharply in a climbing turn and disappeared over the trees.

In the bushes the Chinese spoke softly. They lay on their backs and massaged each other's legs. They attempted to smile at him, but he ignored them and walked to one side and thus claimed the most concealing bush for himself. He turned his back on the general direction of Cuba.

The brush was more rampant than he had thought. Sand contrived to enter the rips between the soles and the uppers of his left shoe. Even the sun put unnatural pressure upon the top of his head, for the checkered, billed cap he had worn from home and through all of Austria and Alsace and had carried through the waterfront streets of most of Europe was now in Rhave's car . . . along with the brown paper bundle and all of the Chinese luggage. He had assumed from the daily papers, through all those years, that Miami was *all* city, with tourists and the rich ones who would leave a car unlocked at night. The habits of all the years of being "displaced" asserted themselves: he crouched behind his own bush. He daydreamed a little, but then remembered how the detective, dressed as a woman, had caught him once in the suburbs of Vienna—well, there were other ways. . . .

V

At noon the green sedan came quietly along the hedge. He had heard tires on the packed coral, had alerted the Chinese with a tossed pebble.

The sedan stopped at an exact spot: the silver hub caps were at the level of his eyes, shining through leaves. The horn sounded once again, more urgently. The Chinese stood up and walked—very much like chorus girls going on the stage —into the back seat of the car. The doors slammed. The car

drove on down the unfinished boulevard. Instead of clearing
the hedge in a climbing turn, it drove and disappeared like an
apparition toward the Federal jail.

After a while, he followed the wheel marks of the yellow
airplane that vaulted the hedge, and of the sedan that rolled a
mile along this "development" near the city's edge. At first,
the signs were no higher than his knees: Estates! Keep an
Eye on *Your* Home! The signs became higher than his head:
Kiwanis: Rotary on Thursday. Then billboards—he was a
failure before their slogans: what Pause was to Refresh him?
How Lucky could he Strike it. . . .

A police car turned into this narrow coral road. He ducked
between the tin and paper breasts of a starlet—a giantess
above him, smiling into the weeds.

Through the latticework under the billboard he watched
the car loiter past. It was a taxi—well, he would learn. Give
him twenty-four hours in any town and he'd know the police
cars. . . .

The habit of rest, the custom of siesta, or the confinement
in a cell where one wears the cloth of indifference was upon
him. The protected cranny below the starlet's blonde smile
and exposed midriff was warm, withdrawn, so he slept.

Toward early evening a piece of tumbling newspaper
awakened him: he emerged from the matted weeds under the
billboard and crawled upon the road, then stood erect and
walked toward the city. Oh, the women with easily opened
purses (in a crowd) would be at the track tomorrow; also,
there would be the ones who could use a discreet, unknown
man to deliver small packets to certain hotel rooms—ah,
Amerika, where the treasure was!

He was all through with this stinking Cuban shirt, the old
dungarees; he was through with Rhave and the police in
Havana who rode free in the taxicabs. He walked into the
first yard where the garage was empty and took a yellow
T-shirt and the beach shorts off the line. He emerged from
the garage looking very much like a tourist, though not
quite so clean. At the next filling station he asked the at-

tendant, "Please. I would appreciate very much a drinkof-water?"

The attendant looked up from the inner tube he was patch-ing and said, "You ought to use our washroom too, mebbe." The attendant got a whiff of him, "Well, how's everything in Sheboygan?"

The skinny man with ears like a horse was already half trotting into the side streets toward the city and the Beach beyond.

Night and the downtown neon flashed new blood into his arms, his fingers. He paused before the windows, for they seemed to display his future: the Copa jackets, with purple slacks: shoes black and white with pointed toes. Someday a zircon ring big as a peach for the second finger. . . .

He laughed so loudly and so suddenly that two ladies from Asheville moved on. He remembered those Chinese. They were in a cell now; *he* was in the street! He sat down on the curb—held his sides. The way they walked into the Border Patrol's car. A line of coolies! But *he* had seen one square-toed, polished black shoe when the front door of the honking car opened. A policeman's foot and a policeman's shoe, the world over. Someone in Polaco town had informed again: the Border Patrol had picked up the pilot's wife; she had told them just to honk at the bushes. But *he* had beaten them again. After a while he got up, strong enough now to walk down the street toward the biggest restaurant in town.

Except he ended up near the city docks at the E-Z Eats, where the menu said Steaks and Chops, and in larger print, No Rough Stuff, Jack, Or Out You Go!

VI

Only the counter was between him and this woman: an acre of starched uniform—an iceberg—above him, the arms crossed. The arms bulged unnaturally, like a man's. Perhaps once she had a bosom, but that had slipped down: the bare arms, and even her flattened nose seemed muscle: she had given up a corset three years ago in Philadelphia.

"Oh, so *now* you don't drink?"

He looked at her.

He wanted to ask the prices, first: he would have the steak and the chop tomorrow maybe. Though he had vowed never to eat fish again in any form once he made the States, the old habit of saving a penny asserted itself even in this place.

"I ast *you* a question." Dolly pushed her waist heavily against the counter, as though to crush him.

"Jack, *everybody* has a drink at E-Z Eats."

This sounded like a statement of fact, as though it were a Miami city ordinance, or her own personal law. In fact, it was a threat.

Well, he believed he would. Yes. Perhaps a glass of wine. Some Sauterne? *au Seltz?*

She did not smile.

She reached under the counter and set a pony of the liquor she had already poured when he walked in off the street. She could tell a man who wanted a drink a mile away. Besides she got a cut on everything she poured. She watched him closely, her face very near his, until he drank her whisky.

Then she was at him again:

"Now you can eat. Steak or chop?"

He didn't know. He really did not know. He'd order in a minute, and was there a . . . near . . . ?

"Oh no you don't!" She reached one long arm across the bar and like some crane at the dockside that toys with a puny boxcar, she sat him forcefully and absolutely back on his stool. Then she shook him like a box of Crackerjack, to settle him in place. Finally, she let go of the handful of cloth on the front of the shirt she had used as a handle.

"Menu," she said impatiently. She placed her finger on the E-Z special: Blue Ribbon K. C. w/coleslaw @ $5.55.

Above him on the back bar the Coca-Cola girls and the cigarette girls with all their charm, smiled down upon the long, flat, Formica bar. He looked past Dolly and into the wide mirror that reflected all of her hips. The Beach seemed as far away as all the States had ever been. Here in the E-Z Lunch was another Miss America, her finger pointing with impatience at the menu.

Well yes. He would certainly order now. He'd have this fish, *au tartar?*

She snatched the menu out of his hand. She threw it flatly on the counter beside his whisky glass. He reeled in the wind.

"Give 'em the swordfish, Tony," she yelled into the small window that opened in on the grill.

Tony's face came into the window, as though his image had been flashed suddenly and angrily upon a screen.

"Swordfish! Swordfeesh!"

His cleaver hammered on the window sill. The door from the kitchen opened. Dolly met him at the pop cooler.

"You lay off a customer—you wop."

After what seemed a very long time, she put a sullen fish in front of him. He did not look at her.

"Don't they say 'Thanks' where you come from, Jack?"

Oh yes. Yes indeed they did. But he wasn't well. He wasn't well. He wasn't really.

"You eat *that*," she commanded, as though it would cure anything.

He tried to eat.

She was trying to bully him: "Where did you come in from, and what's your business . . . wearing them shorts and all?"

Well, he was here on business and . . .

He could not swallow the fish.

Oh yes, he told Dolly, this particular swordfish was very excellent. He said his belly hurt, but secretly he knew it was something else; perhaps if he had one, after all these years, it would be his heart. He could not look at the mermaids on the back bar, though outside beyond the awning's scalloped edge the music, the gambling, the really international set, reflected in neon upon the lowering clouds. A searchlight, probably in front of a restaurant, was his beacon to that *Amerika* of his dreams: it was only one more short walk across a causeway, one more entry, and there he could find a place to sleep . . . no, not in a park.

He was very tired, and the last miles to The Beach beyond were too much. He looked up, but decided not to ask if dessert was included.

"Now ain't I seen you around the tracks?" Dolly had settled all of her hips on top of the pop cooler. She relaxed there to stare at him while she punched at her gums with a gold toothpick.

"At Belmont, I seen you," she said as though she were reading some final charge to the jury. "I never forget a face."

There was no way to explain about the race tracks in Europe. He could not say he had *never* been to the States before this morning. He nodded and looked at the fish. He wondered if the skin was luminous, in the dark.

She shifted all of her weight, and slid off the pop cooler. She walked suddenly—as though she were inspired—to the telephone. She said something into the phone he could not hear. Then hung up.

He was paying for the meal he could not eat, was estimating how little she would let him keep from his last piece of currency. She grabbed the money, turned toward the cash register.

As she turned away the police car stopped at the curb.

With profound relief he saw they had come for him. He was glad: the old routine of fingerprints, the warm cell, the hot meal, the quick deportation to Havana: ah, the Malecon, the beautiful Prado, the siestas, the real life for someone who was maybe too old now to make the Big Success. Rhave would fix it. Was obliged to. And there would always be the tourists who would always need the Guide to show them where the girls were.

So, like a man slipping into a warm bath, he ran from her and from his change, entered the rear seat of the police car more eagerly than the Chinese had done.

The two cops completely ignored him.

They wanted their regular coffee. Delivered to the curb. They honked again. They didn't have all night.

"I hear you, Meatheads!" Dolly called from behind the counter.

She brought out the two paper cups and the driver policeman said nothing except, "Who's that?"

"A cheap bastard," she said and threw the two seventy-five in change into the back seat where the little man was shivering in the Florida night air.

"I just made a *personal* telephone call and he—the little tout—ran out here. You can have him."

The two policemen finished the coffee at their leisure. The driver placed the two empty cardboard cups in the glove compartment, for he always took such things home to his children.

"Now what's this all about," the younger policeman said into the back seat as though he were once again on duty. Dolly was still erect at the curb, waiting to hear what everyone said.

From the back seat the man in the beach shorts said feebly, "*Habana*": Ah, Havana, Cuba.

"Well, if he *don't* like it here!"

Dolly yelled at the closed sedan, but the car was already in the crawling beast of traffic, driving to headquarters.

Czlau raised his head and looked back through the rear window at the restaurant where he had known his moment of freedom. He saw her standing solidly upon her curb, like a vast white abutment in the night.

While Going Down
the Road

While Going Down
the Road

In the side yard beyond the village edge the Doctor saw his father waiting in the rock garden, one hand on the rim of a birdbath.

The Doctor steered up the land. Beyond his windshield he saw the barnyard, the outcrop of rocks in the back pasture, the stonecrop sky. Each year the Doctor had watched the home place atrophy a little. Long ago his father had let her rock garden go to weeds. Blue jays lacerated the overhead branches of pine trees in the front yard. The Doctor confirmed what he had suspected: not yet ready to leave.

Whoaaa, hoss! the old man called across the fence to the automobile. Obediently, but not quite like a black horse, the car stopped. Not packed, not ready to leave. Had his father ever been ready for anything useful?

Still, the Doctor had anticipated some delay and therefore felt he knew the outcome: within two hours, as a matter of family management, he would take his father away from this home place and the old man would then live in the city. . . . Take him away? The Doctor thought of death, that catastrophe that was both his livelihood and his own life's work.

Only last week the Doctor watched the country-style auction. Past noon the auctioneer in his cornhusk of a felt hat led the interested parties from the chicken house, past the corncrib, and into the barn; finally the auctioneer came out through another barn door and the studious men in light biscuit-colored jackets followed the auctioneer in his famous old hat, followed through the rock garden, and through every room of that indifferent house. A final inspection of the premises was customary even though the interested parties already had cruised the line fences, had kicked stones from the pasture, had estimated the long bulge of clay athwart the back forty, and had seen not much at all nearer the creek.

In the center of the barnyard, standing on a square-oak butcher block, the auctioneer cried the land and the house. The interested parties were now a part of the crowd, or they leaned their backs against the corncrib. Farmers who owned land adjoining started the bidding at a fair price, but low. The auctioneer with his famous old felt hat and with his cane and with his sucking peg of a voice worked their top price even higher and at the end of fifty minutes cried out like a prophet.

"Ten dollaha moaha, or Boys I'm a-going to buy her myself.

Once!

"Now boys, doahn't let me do it to myself—do I hear a-hunnrunt and ninety two dollahs and you'll live to re-gret it because

Twice!

"Gentlemun, hits land, and hits

A-sold!"

There was a moment of silence. The varnished cane raised in the sunshine. Fell. Then all of the interested parties nodded, the house had changed hands, had gone to a man said to have bid for still another party as yet unknown. But the high man nevertheless deposited a certified check with the auction-eer's clerk, and some who were not interested parties at all said the price was a little more than the Old Billy Farnham Place would ever be worth.

The Doctor had watched it all. He had seen the house and the ridge of clay on the back forty acres turn into a certified check, a piece of paper; he would invest it wisely and would get still another piece of paper. A check or a prescription blank was a thing he could manage well. The Doctor felt re-lieved. He stood at the crowd's edge and watched the auction-eer's varnished cane flail the sunshine: he heard the auctioneer's forthright, shucking peg voice work through a bushel basket of dishes, then household furnishings, then buckets, four pairs of cow hobbles, a cream separator. To-ward nightfall even the corncrib slouched on its own sled runners was sold to a man who had come here with the others to get what he could get from the Old Billy Farnham Place— well known.

During the week, while the Doctor managed his general practice in Terrace Park, the country people returned to haul everything away. Now the Old Billy Farnham Place lay stripped and supine beneath the clouds of winter running fast overhead. . . . Take him, his father, away? Oh, of course you couldn't just cart the old man off. He wouldn't do that.

Framed between two gate pickets, one hand resting on the rim of a birdbath, his father waited: not yet touched, ap-parently, by the whole plan. Oh, he was there all right: hair white, still perfectly roached, dentures smiling in the plaster cast of his face. Lively enough in the way of so many old traveling salesmen. But not yet packed to leave.

The Doctor walked through the half-open gate. He walked across the yard out into her old rock garden to take a closer look. He noted at once that his father had lost more weight. And there were more saffron blotches beneath the eyes . . .

In the way of father and son, and in the way of two men of two different worlds, they shook hands.

Their hands clasped. The Doctor felt again his old resentments—not that such things mattered any more.

"Why Dad, you're looking well!"

"You tellin' me, Doc?"

What had once been only a trait in his father's speech had now become the whole man. Or had his father's speech always been the voice of straw in the stables of a hundred veterinarians, the voice of a thousand country drugstores in those hamlets of the Middle West. His father's banter was the squeak of buggy wheels, was the flap of side curtains on a dozen Model-T Fords abandoned now along the side roads and short cuts and detours of his father's past. There was something inefficient and wasteful and undirected and shameful about all those years. Had his own father spoken a single sentence in his whole life that was not chatter?

"Making any money, Doc?"

The Doctor was forced to wink, to go along with it. A knowing, melodramatic wink was his sole defense against vulgarity. Still the Doctor managed to place his two white curved fingers on his father's wrist. Professionally, the Doctor concentrated, head tilted to one side. With his finger tips he listened to blood surging like dogs unleashed along an old artery, that old trail for blood just beneath the skin.

"Sound as Farmer Brown's off-mare," the old man said without listening to the thing his only son might have told him. "Skinny as a rail, and eat like a blind dog in a meat house. That's a fact."

The Doctor said nothing.

To get on with it, to set an example, the Doctor turned toward a side door of the house where once the three of them had lived—you could call it that—had lived together. Since the day of the auction sale the house had been nearly vacant. Now their footsteps and their voices re-echoed in the empty rooms. Yet his father could not accept this necessary change. Therefore, to jolly the old man along, the Doctor spoke again in the voice of false cheer that he so despised in others.

"Right," the Doctor said. Oh, he knew his father was a dying man. "Right, Dad. Right as rain."

The stove and the kitchen cabinet had been carted away. Only the old smells seemed to hang like cinnamon-colored bats from the ceiling and all along the kitchen walls: the odor of nutmeg, of split wood, of used jar rings, the odor of mold congealed behind the wainscot.

By contrast the Doctor thought of his own inner rooms of his own clinic in Terrace Park: those walls painted beige each year, enameled pans white as a bandage. The patients who came there were neither brothers nor strangers nor friends; they were merely patients who needed his and only his help. They were the white, stalklike bodies supine on his examination table. Low-voiced questions; the whispered reply. For fever, penicillin, esp. hemolytic streptococci; for certain anemias, iron . . . a prescription folded once, tucked carefully into purse or wallet. Sometimes the Doctor's prodding fingers found the big tumors and then after the routine tests, he went through his little talk, which said, "Having lived a rich life, and having raised your family, and all . . ." To say these things was his duty, his obligation; it gave him satisfaction. He had made the little talks so many times he was now, in fact, the kind of person he had always wanted to become.

His father surprised him.

"I'll pack a few things, Doc. Then skiddoo."

Nimbly the old man vanished into the bedroom. Closed the door. Private.

Behind the bedroom door, the Doctor heard the two empty suitcases tumble from a closet shelf, and bounce, and then everything was very still.

The Doctor was very pleased, as when a patient made a mysterious, rapid recovery. He was also resentful.

Secretly the Doctor wanted a final show of loyalty from his father. From his father the Doctor wanted a little sentiment about this used-up "farm" and about these rooms where the woman who was wife and mother lived out her days. To get this wish was beyond his conventional skill, but the Doctor, their only child, wanted to legislate repentance; or better still, he wanted to see evidence of regret. He might finally settle for piety, or that failing he was willing to accept a prompt departure as a symptom of . . . well, something. Instead, the Doctor heard his father's cheerful, almost obscene voice singing behind the bedroom door:

. . . *Skiddoo, skiddoo, skid-skid, skiddooo with you—*

The Doctor turned his face from the bedroom door and he saw the lighter patch of hyacinth-flowered wallpaper where her piano stood until last week's auction.

The piano was gone, taken away for the use of a farmer's young wife, a woman who did not play at all but who had a place for an old upright in her living room. Now the upright patch of wallpaper was scar tissue, pale and stretched thin against the wall.

When young, before her marriage, the Doctor's mother once studied piano almost a year at the Cincinnati Conservatory of Music. Then she married and began to teach piano students of her own. His mother's students walked across the iron bridge from the village: girls in middy blouses, or girls in dresses of flowered print. They came to the door with a black music roll in one hand and fifty cents tied in a handkerchief. For a full hour it was *two-three-four* and it was "keep our wrists arched." It was *Country Gardens* and *Southern Roses Waltz*; it was *Barcarole* in the afternoon, and on into the sterile night. The Doctor had seen a hairbrush perched on a fat wrist: "We must keep our fingers free. Free!"

All that time he had studied in the kitchen, the door almost closed.

After the last student walked back across the iron bridge, and after another cold supper, his father might blow in from Brookings, or Galion, or Upper Sandusky, Ohio.

Hair roached, shoes polished, a watch chain asserting itself across his vest, his father always blew in, and always walked laughing through the house, "Why hell-o everybody! Oh, a great day for ducks in Elkator. Best short ribs in the U.S.A.

at Peter Vort's (Dutchman, nice fellow) just outside Hib-
blings, Minney-shota. Howsa boy, Harry? Still grinding
away at the old books? *Goooood*."

His mother had put up with it and the Doctor never understood her reasons. As a boy he had felt too much alone to
care, and now he was too busy to want to understand. That
was about it.

From behind what had once been his mother and father's
bedroom door, silence. No tantrum of packing. Was anything
left in this vacant house that was worth the packing?

To get on with it, the Doctor opened their old bedroom
door.

His father sat on the bed.

On the floor were two woven-straw suitcases. His father
had spent a lifetime checking out of bad hotels. Now he
could not walk out of an almost empty room. Tears ran
down his father's cheeks.

"Couldn't lift 'em, Doc," he lied. Yet there was a certain
familiar banter in the old voice, and a little shame because of
the tears. "We can't leave, Doc. I'm sick."

The Doctor leaned forward and looked closely at the old
man's face. He saw a subtle, droopy flutter at the corner of
the lip . . . stroke? Abstractly, the Doctor peeled up the lid
of his father's eye. He focused on the thin, scattered blood
vessels of the eyeball. Nothing of note. He heard himself say,
"Bit odd, that . . ."

"Still, in that case," the Doctor went on smoothly. "Guess
we can't leave. Guess we can't leave after all."

The old man nodded. He looked better at once.

"But also," the Doctor said professionally, "we had better
just have a good look."

Quickly the Doctor went out to his black sedan and returned with a black, upholstered bag. Certain things he always carried along in the automobile, even for city driving.

Very willingly, almost eagerly, his father stretched out on
the bed for examination.

For a moment the stethoscope held father and son together.

The Doctor heard the rush of liquid through the resinous old heart. . . . The blood pressure, the cough, *now the right side, please*. No, certainly no cachexia.

Casually, the Doctor's fingers pushed into his father's belly. Without changing expression, he found what he already knew he would find: the liver. Larger now. Not much, but larger just the same. For two years the Doctor had known about this liver. For two long years. This liver was atypical . . . no ascites.

"At your age, Dad," and the Doctor said the necessary lie, "at your age I hope I'm in as good shape. I sure do."

The older man smiled. The Doctor closed in on him.

"Why you're *all* set to go. Let's hit the pike."

Because the old man had once purchased mileage books with the best of them, had carried patent medicines, had finally traveled in seasoning, spice, bulk coffee, and a side line of talcum powder for billiard parlors, because he had what the boys called a real following, the old man got to his feet. When he heard the word Go, he was ready. P.D.Q.

"We got a nice day for it," the old man said brightly, "hey Doc?"

"Right," the Doctor said and he picked up the straw suitcases and led the way toward the kitchen. "Right as rain."

But in the center of the kitchen his father stopped.

The old man grabbed one of the suitcase handles. He balked. He sat down on the corner of the wood box. Tears came again to his father's eyes.

The Doctor felt all his training bind like a wet surgical glove on his hand. Although baffled and angry he said nothing at all. He waited. He stared out the window and into her abandoned rock garden. The neglect of her rock garden, the bankruptcy of the place seemed inexcusable. All of his old resentments came back once more.

"Harry-boy," his father said, "I can't leave her. Can't leave your mother here."

Oh it was an outrage. The Doctor knew it. This stalk of a man had run through his mother's inheritance and after her death had even neglected . . . Hadn't he abandoned her for weeks on end while he "called on" livery stables, small grocery stores, and poolrooms? Now, after a lifetime of this he refused, in her name, to leave this final, open kitchen door. The sentimentality was too much.

The Doctor said nothing. In exasperation he tapped his foot. The tune was about the only music he cared to know, the almost forgotten melody of *Southern Roses Waltz*. Because of his training he tried to put all of the past from his mind. But his father would not permit it.

"You wouldn't know, Doc. What I meant to your mother."

"Oh?" Now he had heard everything. He nodded his head. Interested.

"Used to drink. Some. Us drummers had'a do that."

The old man settled down on the wood box. He remembered it all very well. Like yesterday.

Useta drink. Yes, I did. Why I took on great big jags—like they say. Well, then I met your mother. Harry, you wouldn't know what a fine woman she was. One time and another we talked about it. Then. Well, I up and quit the drink."

The old man clicked his lips, and with his hand made the small motion of turning off a faucet. "Quit the drink. Just like that."

Oh, the case was too clear. The Doctor knew his father was an abstinent man. The facts of the matter were not complicated: at age thirty his father stopped drinking. As a reward for this virtue his mother sometimes forwarded money from the piano lessons to defray his expenses on the road. As a salesman his father just about broke even. Because of this single virtue of abstinence she waited until all hours to welcome him home, to see the watch chain shining across his checkered vest.

"Also, Harry-boy. I could meet the public. Your mother appreciated that."

For the first time the Doctor understood it. He understood the thing she found to admire in his father. For a mo-

ment the Doctor felt more lonely and bereaved than he had
ever felt when his father was away and when he, himself,
was caught between misery and ambition, studying at the
kitchen table, listening to—but not wanting to hear—a girl
with fat wrists hoeing her way through *Country Gardens*.

As an adult, as a man licensed by the State to practice
medicine on others, he could now see it all with a kind of
detachment. His mother had taught only elementary piano
and in her lifetime she had not one distinguished student. In
addition, she could arrange fruits very well in a bowl. Therefore a man could please her merely by naming the hotel
clerks at Washington Court House, or Mount Vernon, Ohio.
His father's ability to "meet the public" stood for all that was
sophisticated in life. As simple as that. . . .

The old man stopped talking.

He misread his son's look of neutral bemusement. He
thought his son's look was more implied criticism.

"Ahhh, you wouldn't know about all that. You was a cold
'un. Nose in a book!"

At last the old man had said what he had always felt. Now,
as always, he felt no match for this touchy, self-contained
general practitioner who was also his son. After all, was a
man who had traveled in patent medicines, who had a real
following, was he so damn different from a regular doctor?
Why you might say they carried the same line. And hadn't
the boy learned a thing or two from him about meeting the
public. Couldn't you say that?

Tears came to the old man's eyes.

"There, there," the Doctor said as though he were treating
a child. "You're feeling just fine, Dad. We both know that."

For the first time the Doctor put his arm around his
father's shoulder. Beneath the old, double-breasted suit coat
he felt a skeleton, his father's bones. Beneath that skin he felt
the roof ridge and the cupolas of all the one-night hotels, and
felt the gravel of country roads, the bricks of railroad plat-
forms, the dormers, the lean-to sheds of country places set
back from the road, the odor of wet harness, of talcum in

billiard parlors . . . all these things beneath the cloth of a suit that came from Montgomery Ward's. . . . And all that time, at home, a sullen boy, his son, reading at the kitchen table, already a little humorless, a little grim . . .

The old man bent—was a weakened stalk. His full weight rested on his son. Like the scratch and the sudden opal light of a match struck against the wall of some abandoned room, the memory of one instant of time past returned to him: it was the night of a fire in the grate, of a rosewood piano in the corner, of a well-lighted room and his own heartfelt, *Hell-o everybody!* No matter how tired, he always came in like that to cheer them up: *A great day for ducks in Elkator.* Then all the news. The memory of that instant was too much. The old man's tears ran down his cheeks and fell and disappeared into the pin stripe of the Doctor's suit. The old-fashioned suitcase of woven straw lay between their feet.

The Doctor knew—professionally—it was over.

He knew he could and so he did lead the old man out of the house and toward the Buick parked in the lane. Management was partly a matter of timing, of course.

Without wanting to, the Doctor felt a little superior.

They stood for a moment beside the car. The old man straightened and looked his son in the eye. He now believed his son was angry at the delay. Well, if there was anything wrong the father wanted to make it right. And because he could still meet the public he said the best thing by way of apology, to make things right.

"Has paid you," the old man said forthrightly, giving full credit where credit was due. "Harry, all that study has surely paid you."

There. He had said it. Was glad. No time for hard feelings before a little trip.

The Doctor said nothing at all. It was not the kind of thing he wanted to hear, but of course it had paid him very well. . . .

In the way of a man who can still meet the public, his

father changed the subject. He looked at the high, steadily enlarging clouds overhead.

"Harry, Old Hoss, we got a nice day for it. Let 'er go!"

Therefore for the last time they drove across the iron bridge at the village edge. The Doctor was glad for they were driving back into his own world. Ahead was his private office, his examination rooms, his nurse. The small farm was behind them. His own past, like a difficult case that had hung on and on, was closed.

His father sat erect. Well, he sure was glad to get out for a nice little drive. Like as not they would meet up with someone he had known in Goshen or Sligo or Frampton's Crossing. Always did because he never forgot a face. . . . Meet a man once, shake his hand, never forget him. *High, Low, Jack, and the Game.*

On the father's side of the Buick a signboard loomed huge in the windshield, then passed suddenly like an apparition. The growl of power from this new black automobile pleased the old man. 'Course never had a real *fine* automobile himself, but rode out many a mileage book—long before your time, Harry. Also had the first Model-T in Harkum Township. No big cars, so never missed them. The fiddle-scrape of an old tune came to mind; he whistled softly between his dentures, *Ohhhh, Buffalo Gals won't you come out to-night.* . . . Funny what you came across in kitchens away out in the country when you are carrying a line of spice or talcum also good for home use. Well, he'd turned down a few, once upon a time . . .

The Doctor glanced at his father who now dozed in the warmth of the car.

The Doctor knew exactly how these cases went. The irony struck him anew: cirrhosis, afflicting a patient not at all alcoholic, who was in fact abstinent as a minor point of virtue. Yet his diagnosis was firm. The splotches of discoloration on the forehead and on the backs of the hands plainly announced what was ahead. The liver would continue to enlarge, of course; the loss of weight would be frightening for the result was a kind of starvation. Amidst all the possibilities of food in the world his father's body could accept none of the right kind. In the end.

The Doctor knew he would use his conventional skill to help his father die well in some final sunlit room—no doubt in the illusion of love. He would do what he could do, with money no real object. It struck the Doctor anew that his work really had paid him well enough. Not as much as some doctors he could name, but enough . . .

On the Doctor's side of the car another signboard loomed, and filled the windshield, and then passed. In spite of his training the Doctor permitted himself to consider what might be the flaw within his own scrubbed, cleverly tailored body. Had he perhaps inherited the same, creeping hepatomegaly? He did not exactly believe he himself was exempt from something. But he thought only, "No. No need to think about that. Not yet . . ."

Suddenly, from half-sleep, the old man raised his head. The old man now seemed very pleased to be going down the road, scything along the highway.

"A wunner-ful day for it Doc. We sure have . . ."

Then his father really was asleep.

The Doctor said nothing at all. He watched the highway unfold in curves and flats and white center lines on Tarvia, or on cement, contained always by the running berms of clay.

For him, ahead, was this identical warm, unfolding afternoon.

In the outer rooms of his clinic the children and men and women would be seated all in rows, crying and playing or looking at old magazines.

And that was about it, for the rest of the day.

Other New Directions—
San Francisco Review Books: